FAR OUT
FAIRY TALES

STONE ARCH BOOKS
a capstone imprint

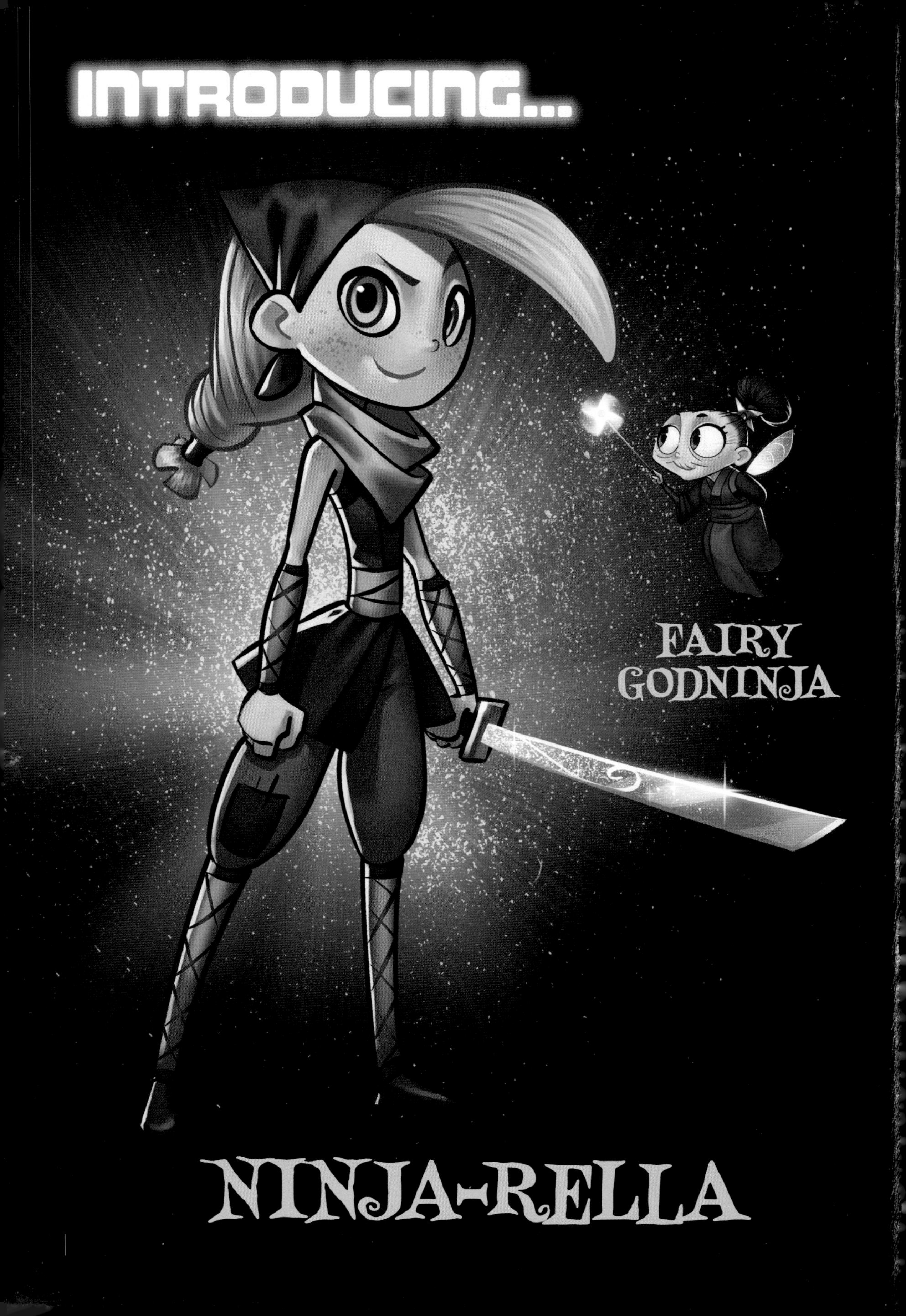
INTRODUCING...
FAIRY GODNINJA
NINJA-RELLA

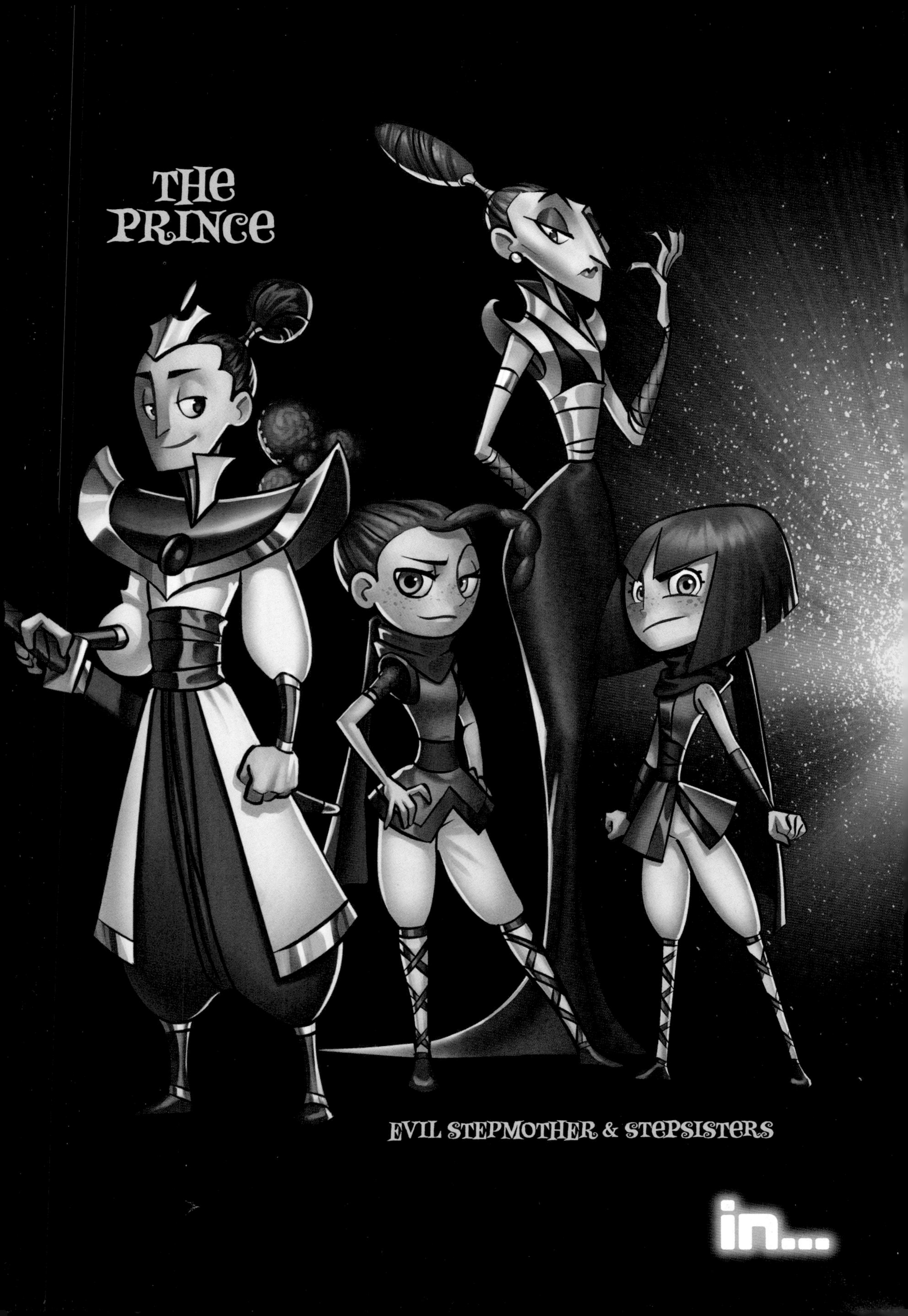
THE PRINCE
EVIL STEPMOTHER & STEPSISTERS
in...

Far Out Fairy Tales is published by
Stone Arch Books
A Capstone Imprint
1710 Roe Crest Drive, North Mankato,
Minnesota 56003
www.capstonepub.com

Cataloging-in-Publication Data is
available at the Library of Congress
website.
Hardcover ISBN: 978-1-4342-9647-4
Paperback ISBN: 978-1-4342-9651-1

Summary: Cinderella's stepmother and
two stepsisters treat her like dirt. But
each night, in secret and in shadows,
Cinderella trains to be a ninja! More
than anything, Cinderella yearns
to become the prince's personal
bodyguard. But how can she meet him
when her stepmother won't ever let
her leave?

Lettering by Jaymes Reed.

Designer: Bob Lentz
Editor: Sean Tulien
Managing Editor: Donald Lemke
Creative Director: Heather Kindseth
Editorial Director: Michael Dahl
Publisher: Ashley C. Andersen Zantop

Printed in the United States of
America in North Mankato, Minnesota.
052019   000080

FAR OUT FAIRY TALES

Ninja-rella

A GRAPHIC NOVEL

BY JOEY COMEAU

ILLUSTRATED BY OMAR LOZANO

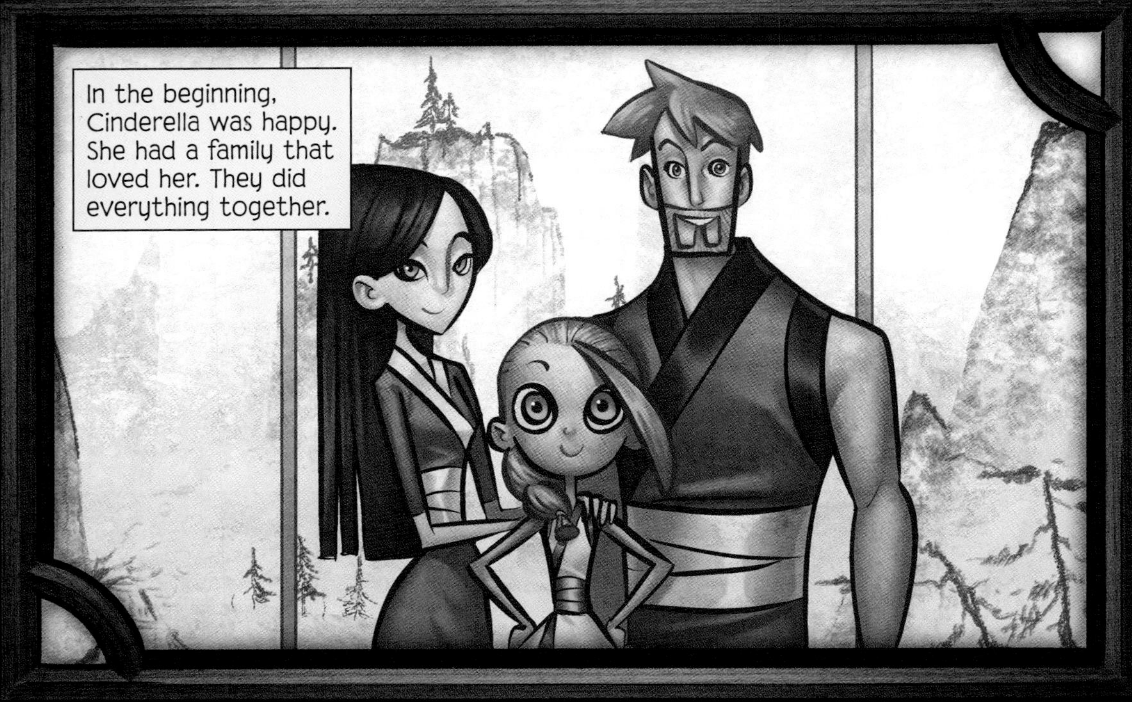
In the beginning, Cinderella was happy. She had a family that loved her. They did everything together.

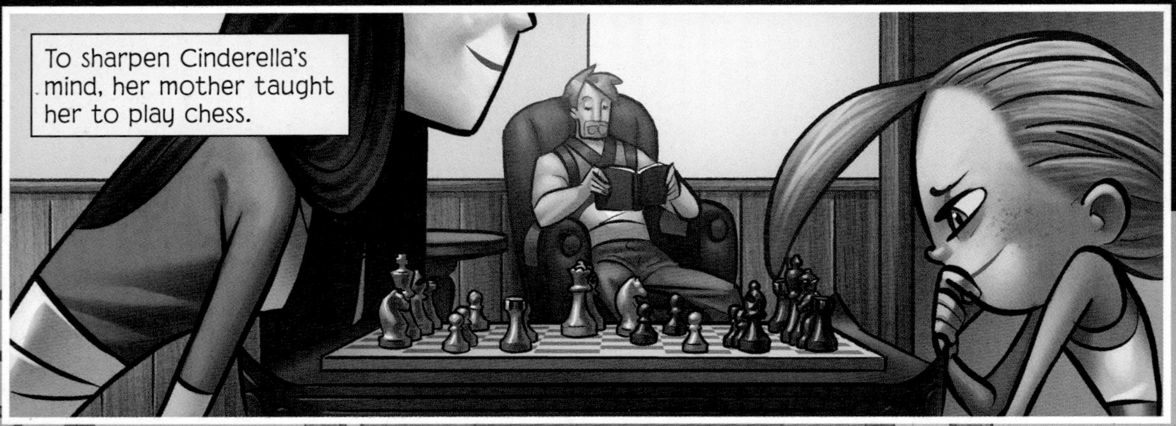
To sharpen Cinderella's mind, her mother taught her to play chess.

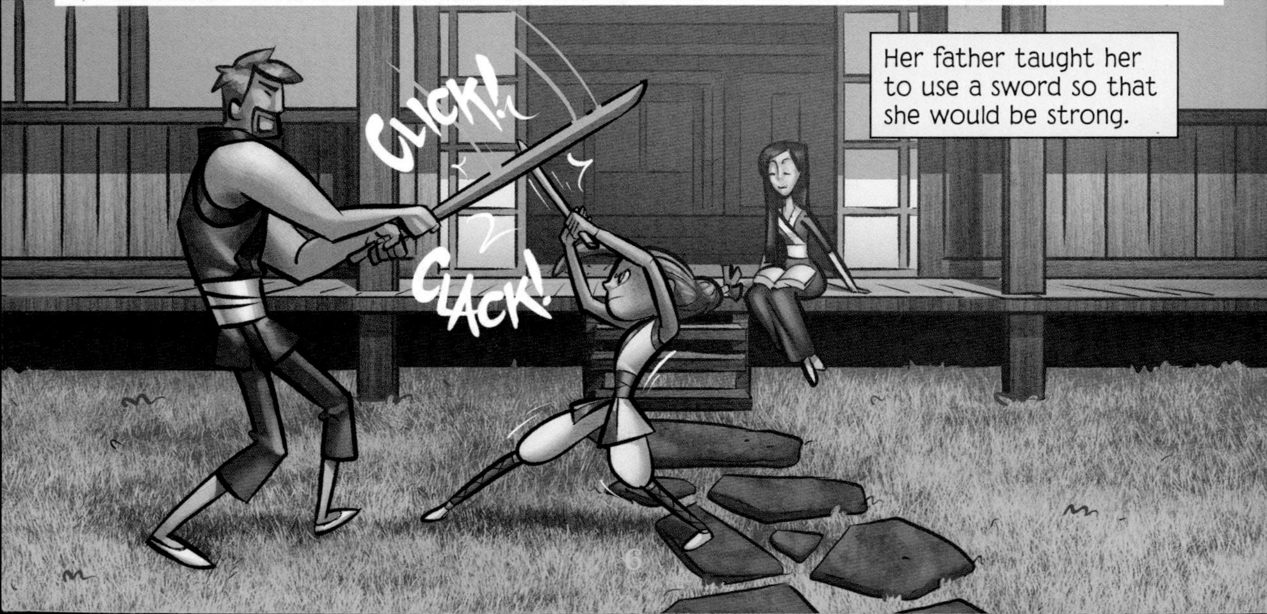
Her father taught her to use a sword so that she would be strong.
CLICK!
CLACK!

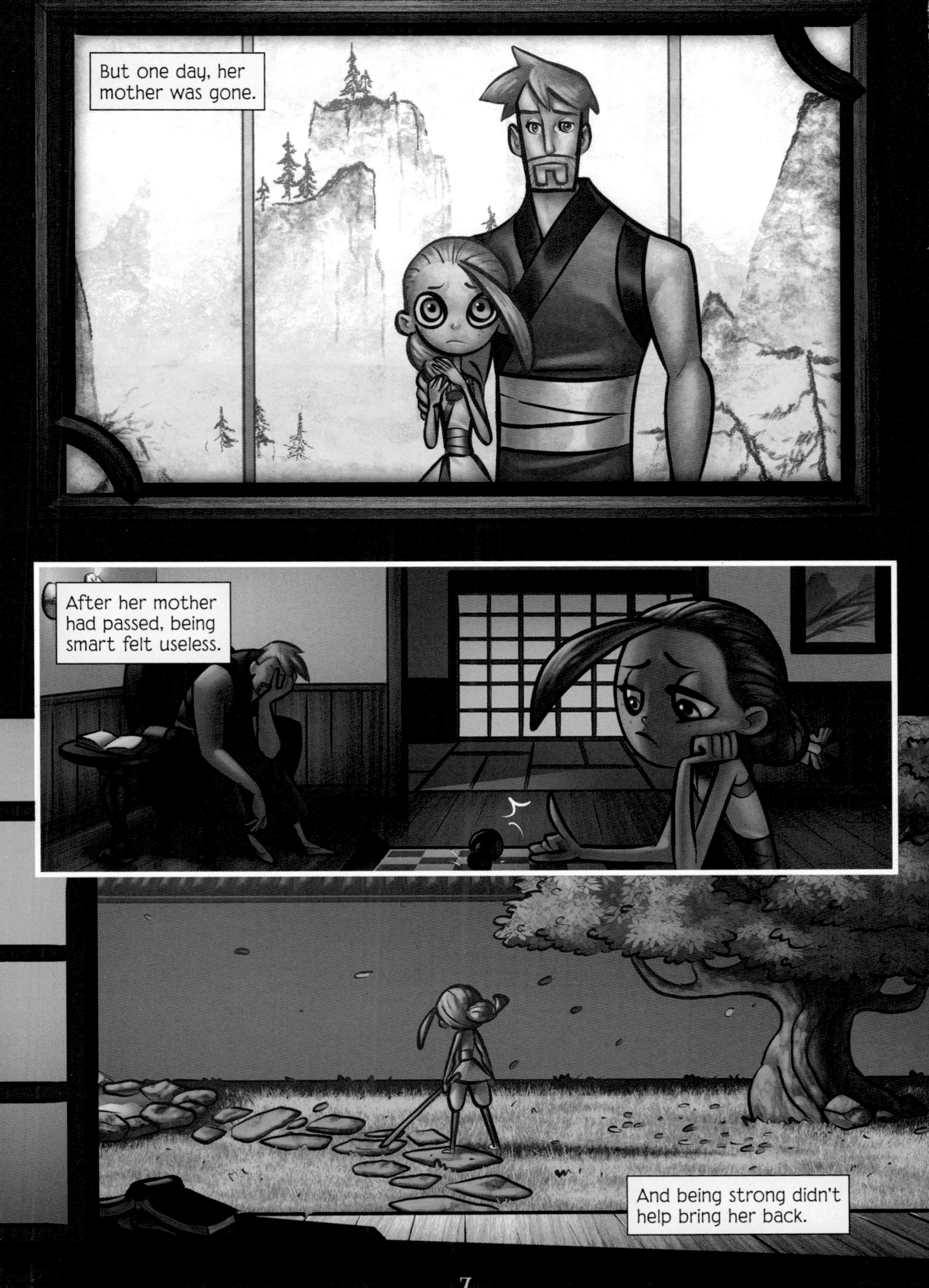
But one day, her mother was gone.
After her mother had passed, being smart felt useless.
And being strong didn't help bring her back.

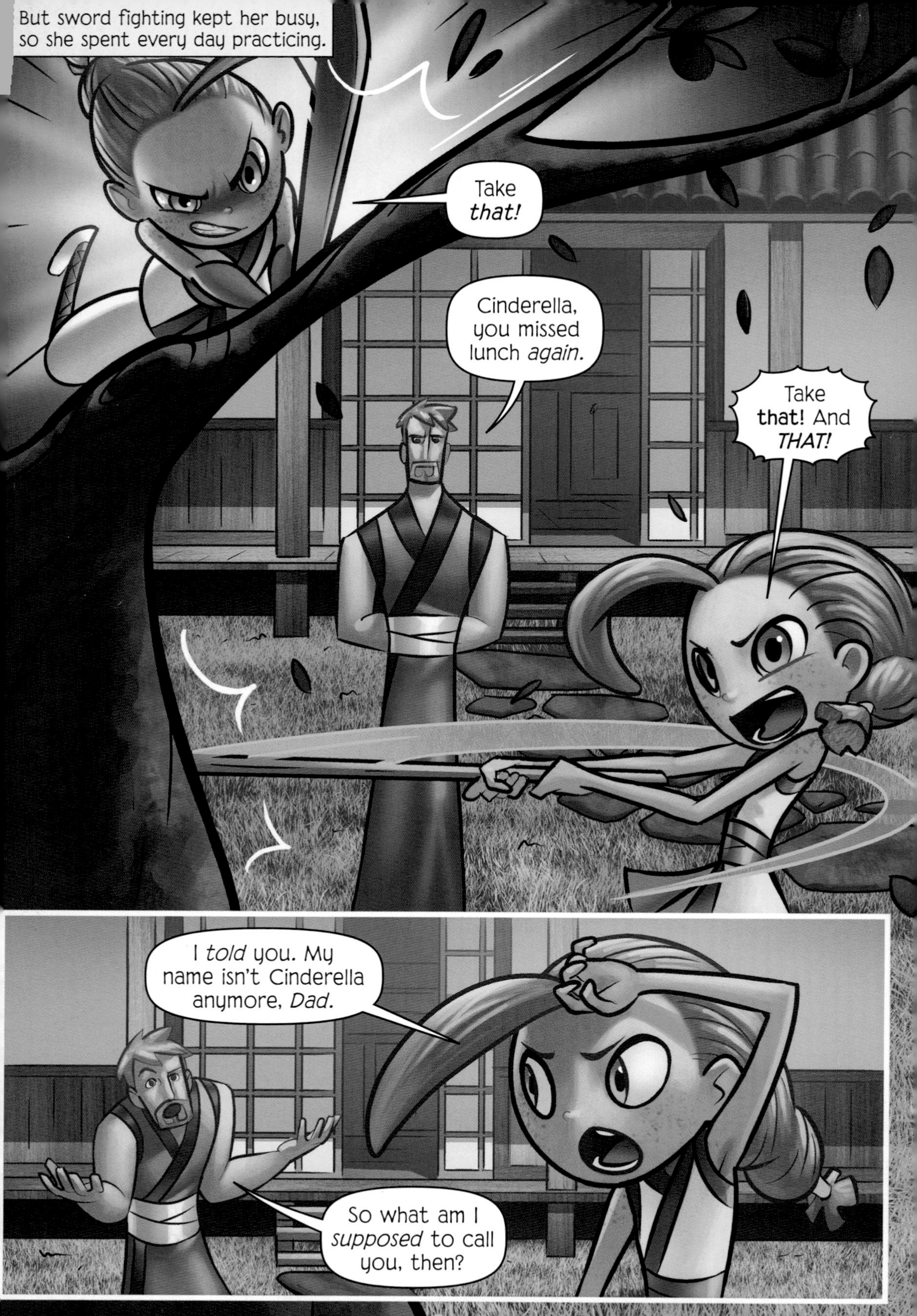
But sword fighting kept her busy, so she spent every day practicing.
Take *that!*
Cinderella, you missed lunch *again.*
Take **that!** And *THAT!*
I *told* you. My name isn't Cinderella anymore, *Dad.*
So what am I *supposed* to call you, then?

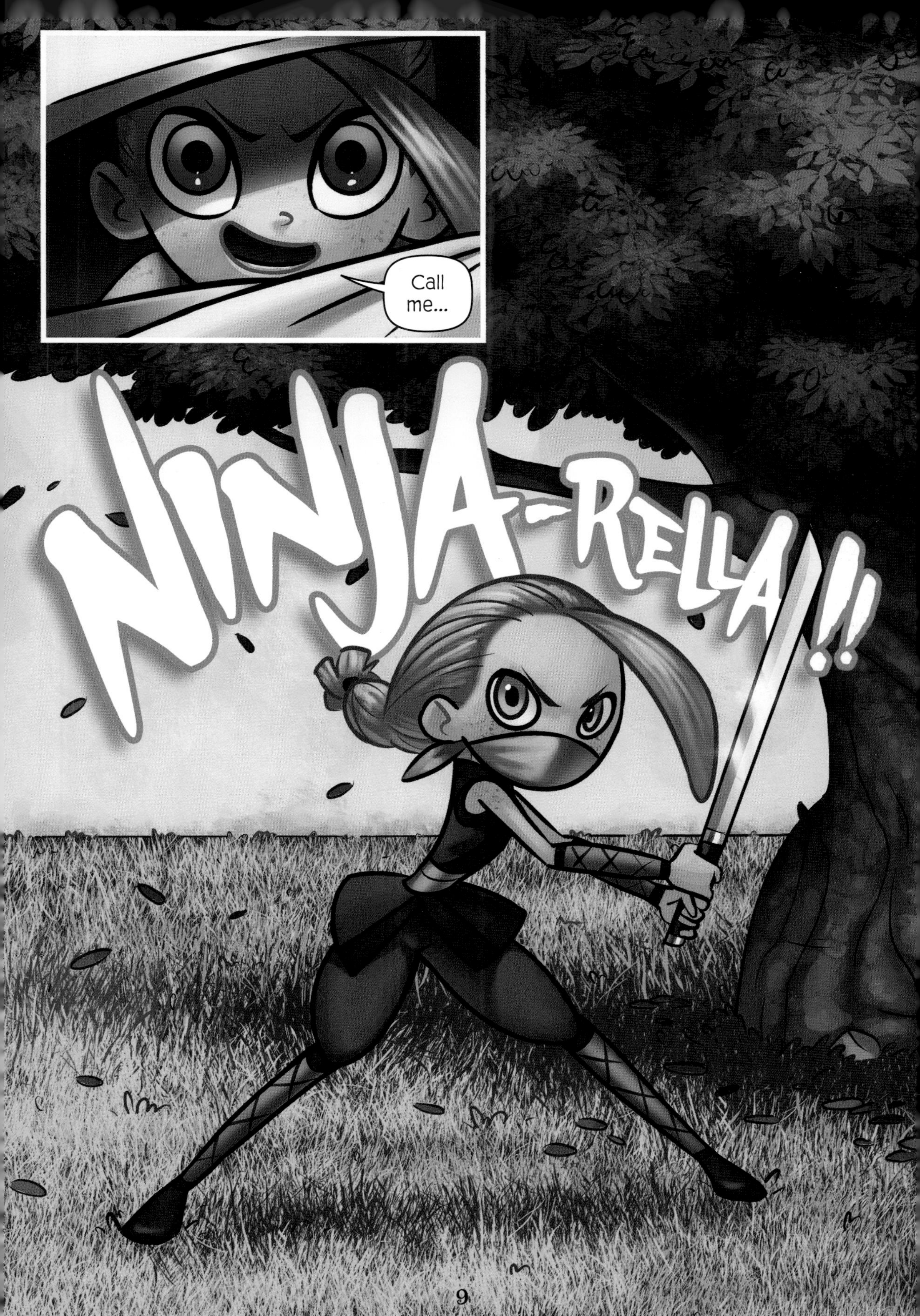
Call me...
NINJA-RELLA!!

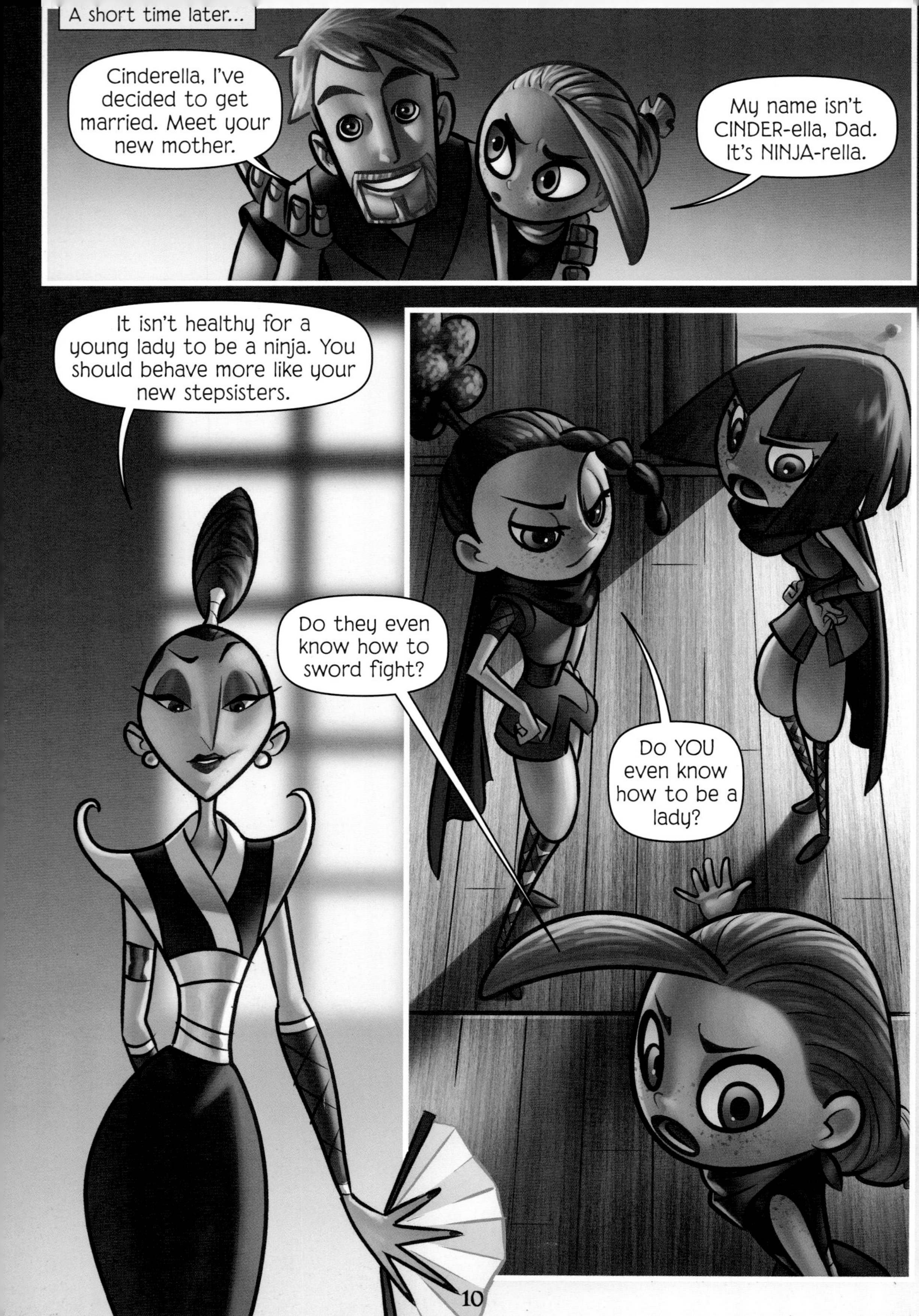
A short time later...
Cinderella, I've decided to get married. Meet your new mother.
My name isn't CINDER-ella, Dad. It's NINJA-rella.
It isn't healthy for a young lady to be a ninja. You should behave more like your new stepsisters.
Do they even know how to sword fight?
Do YOU even know how to be a lady?

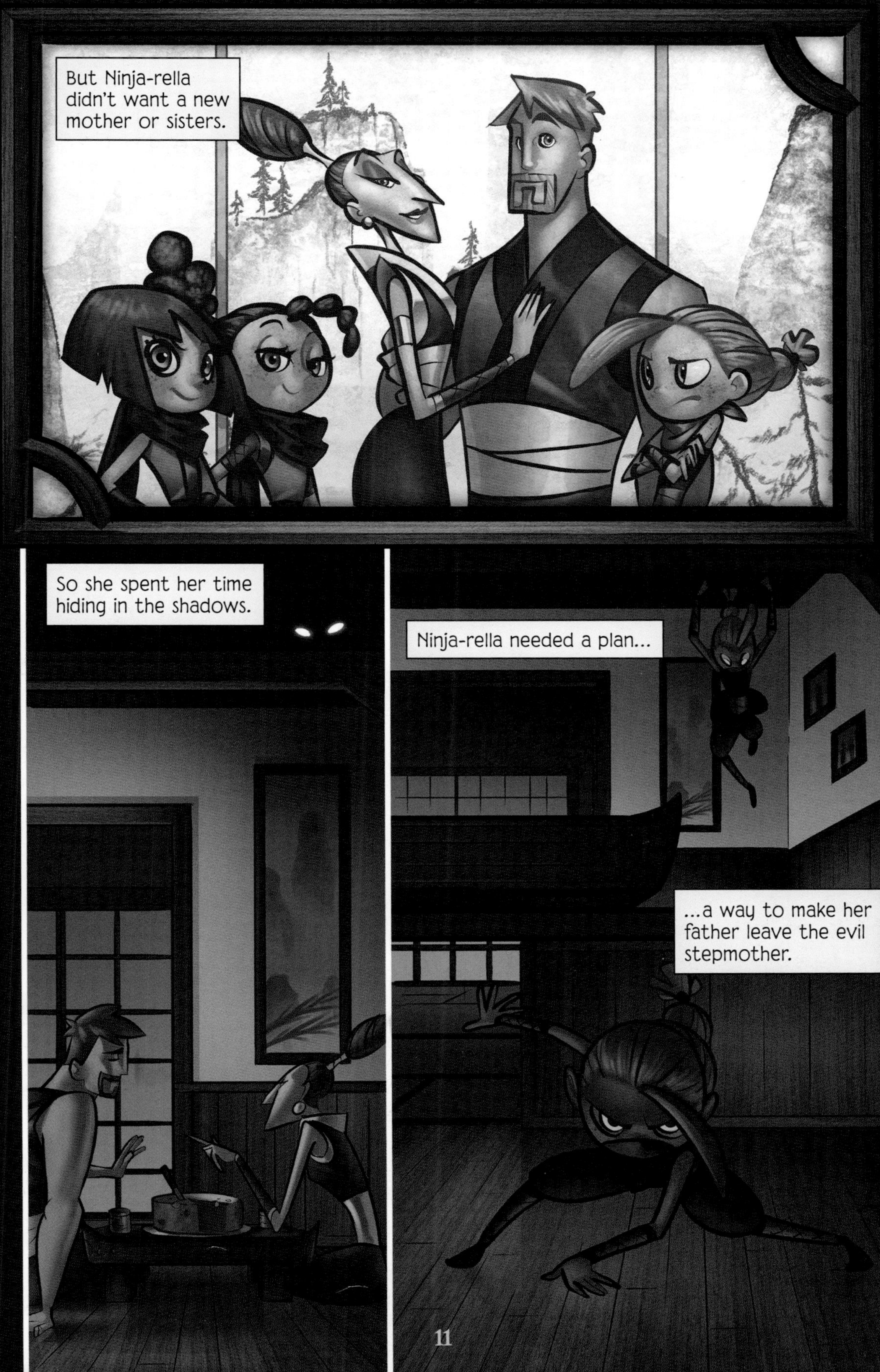
But Ninja-rella didn't want a new mother or sisters.
So she spent her time hiding in the shadows.
Ninja-rella needed a plan...
...a way to make her father leave the evil stepmother.

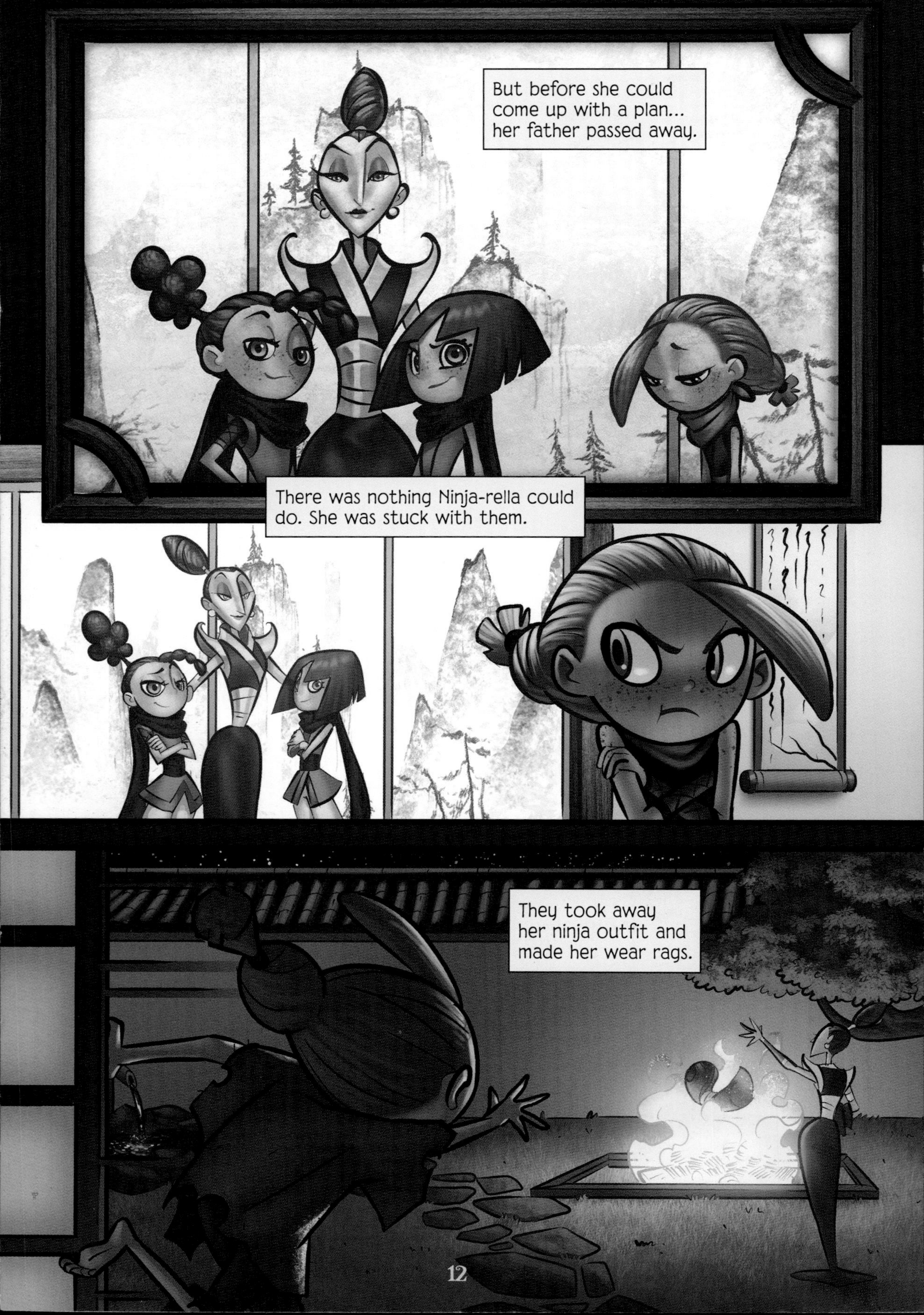
But before she could come up with a plan... her father passed away.
There was nothing Ninja-rella could do. She was stuck with them.
They took away her ninja outfit and made her wear rags.

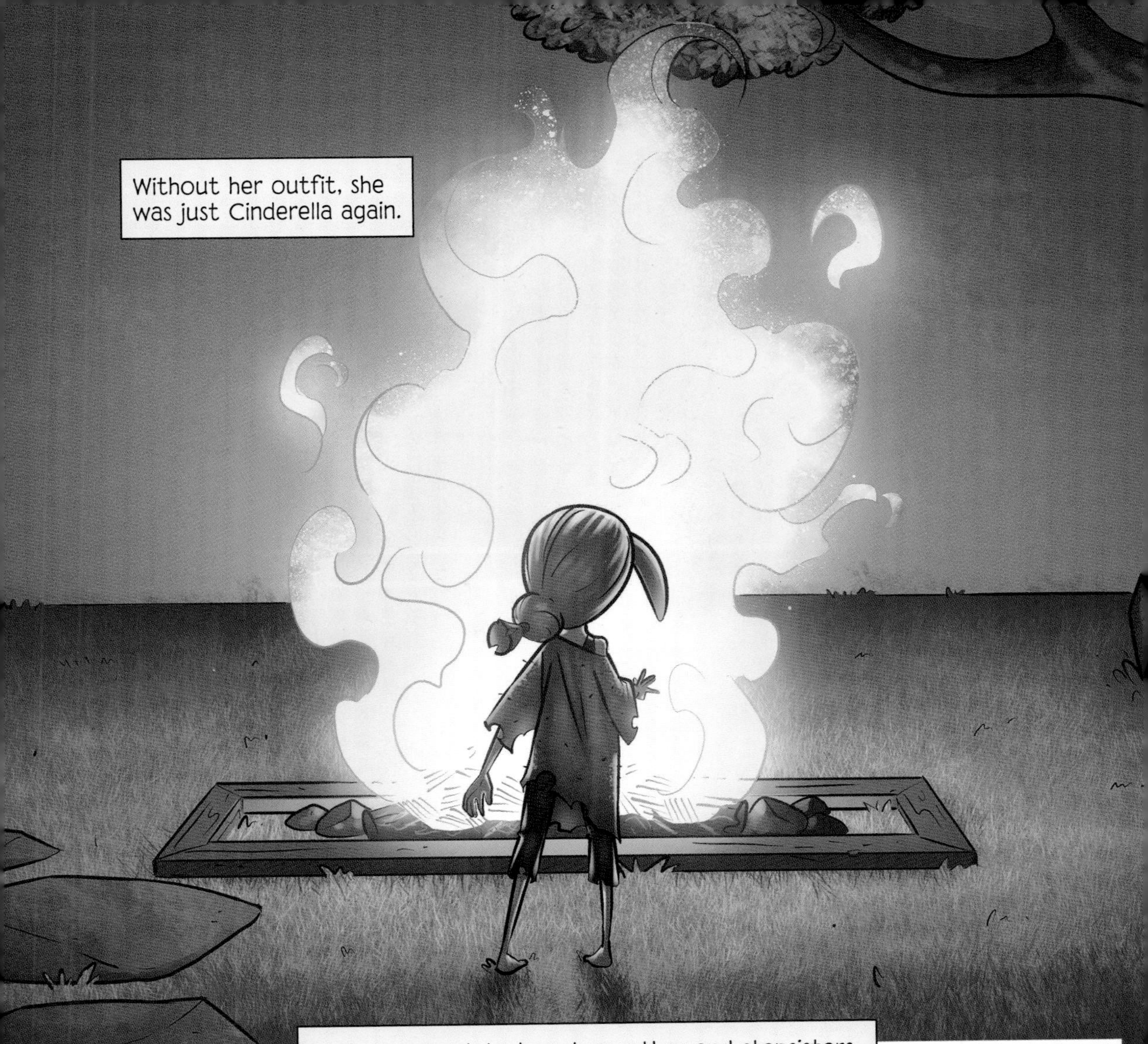
Without her outfit, she
was just Cinderella again.

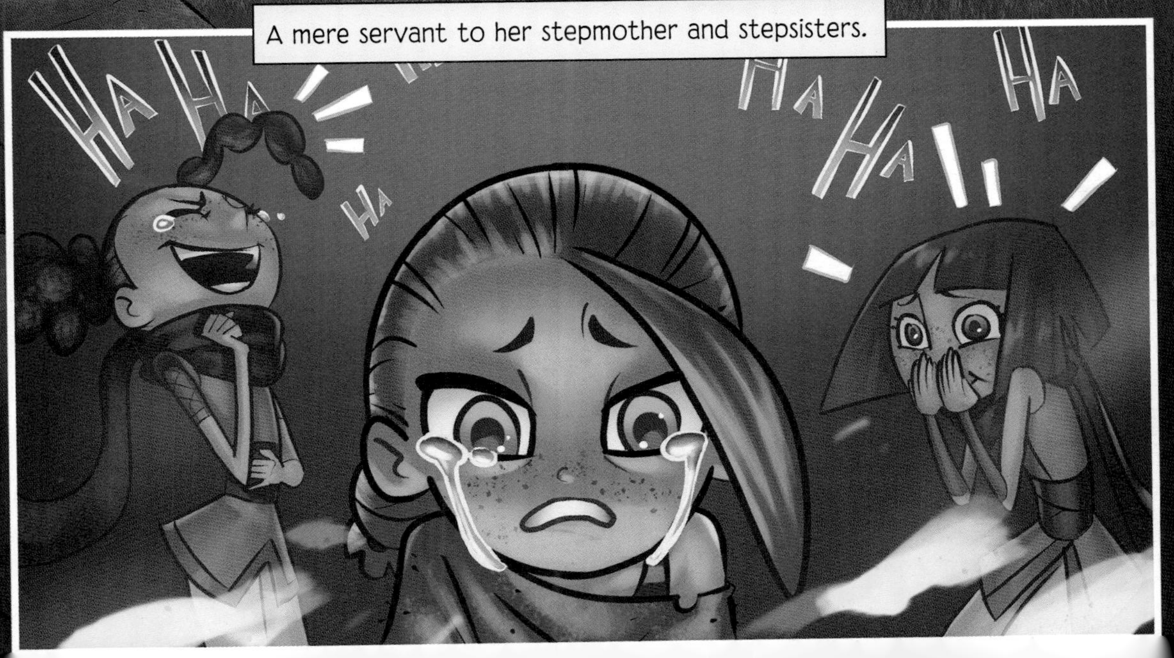
A mere servant to her stepmother and stepsisters.
HA HA HA
HA
HA HA HA
HA

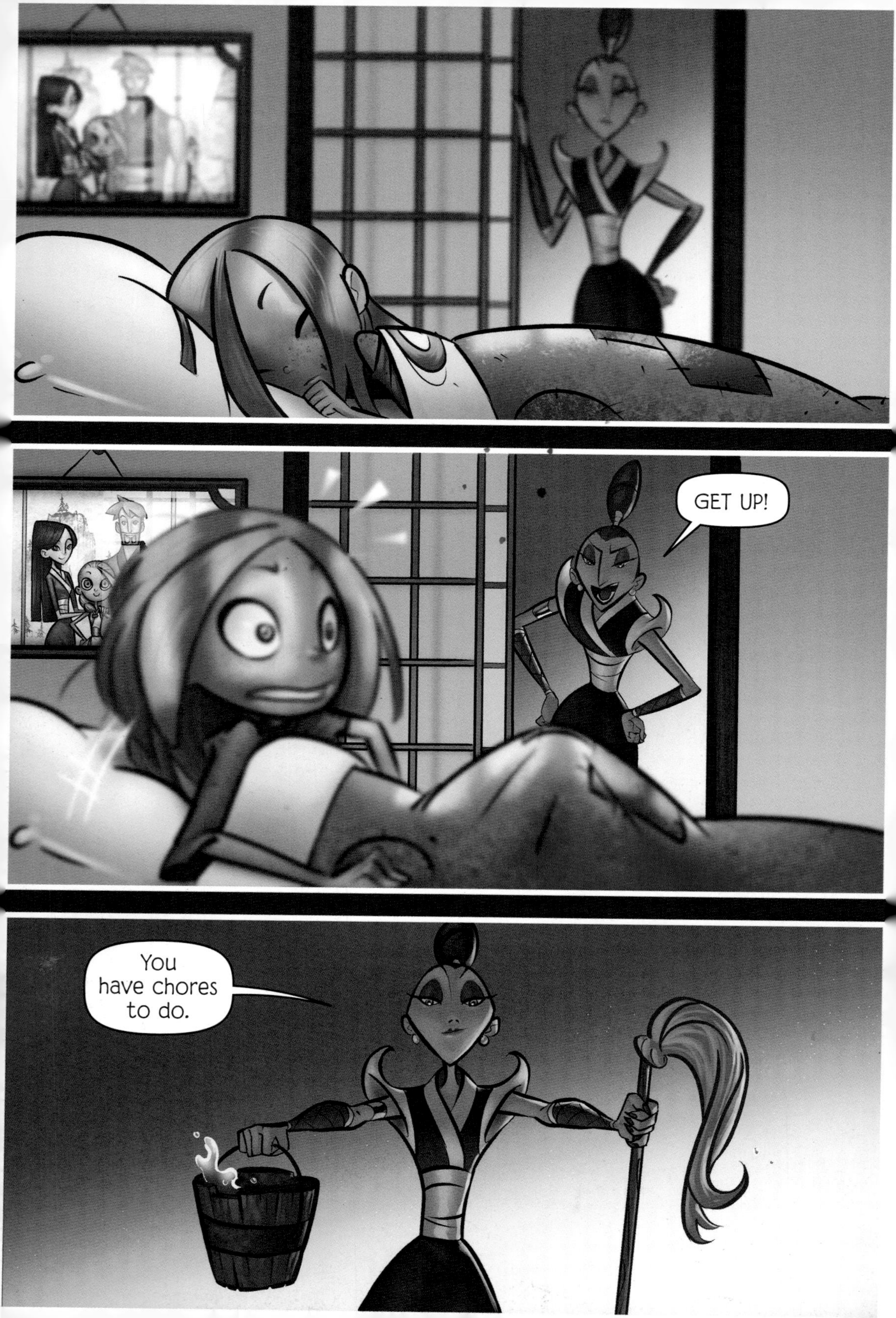
GET UP!
You have chores to do.

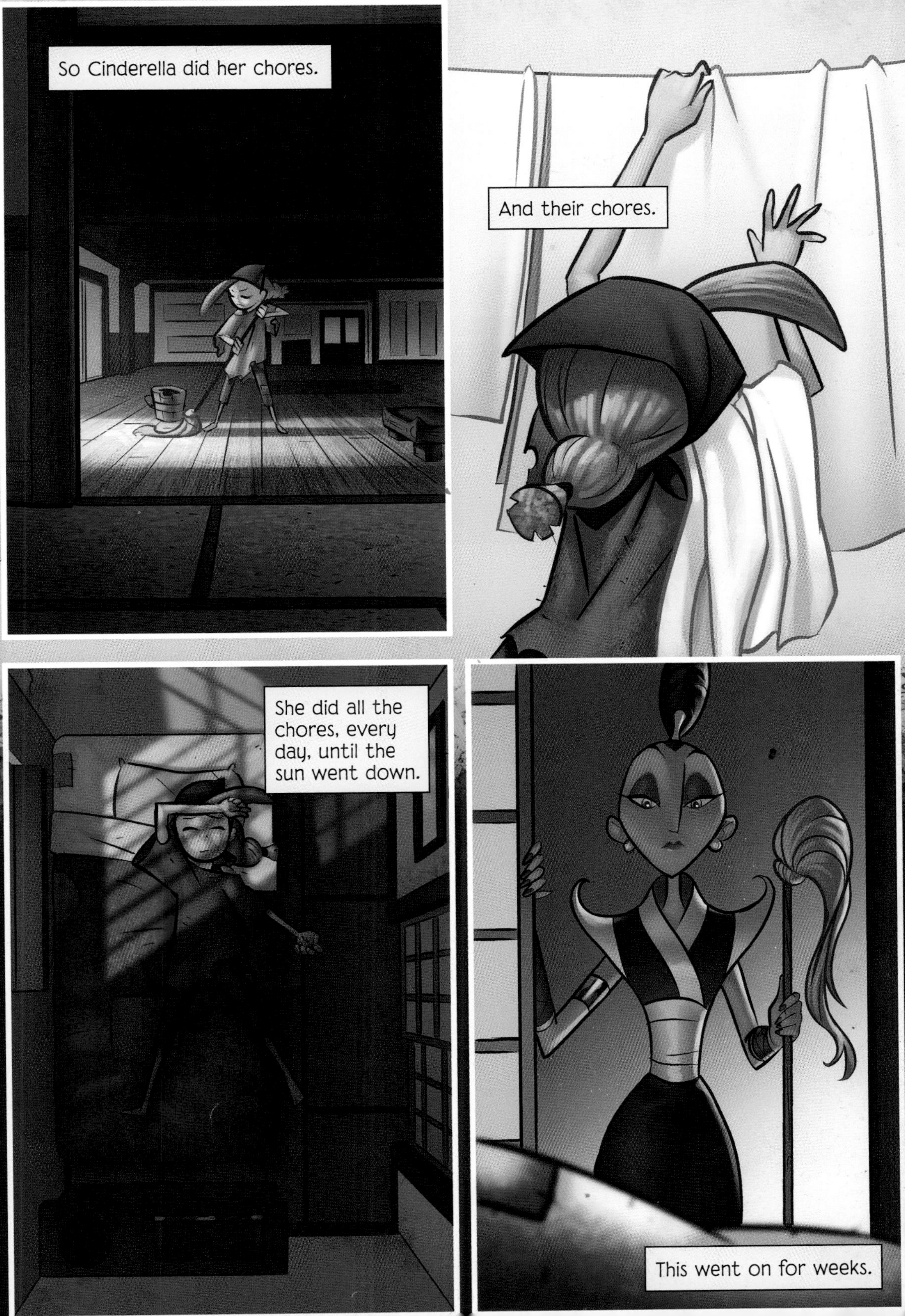
So Cinderella did her chores.
And their chores.
She did all the chores, every day, until the sun went down.
This went on for weeks.

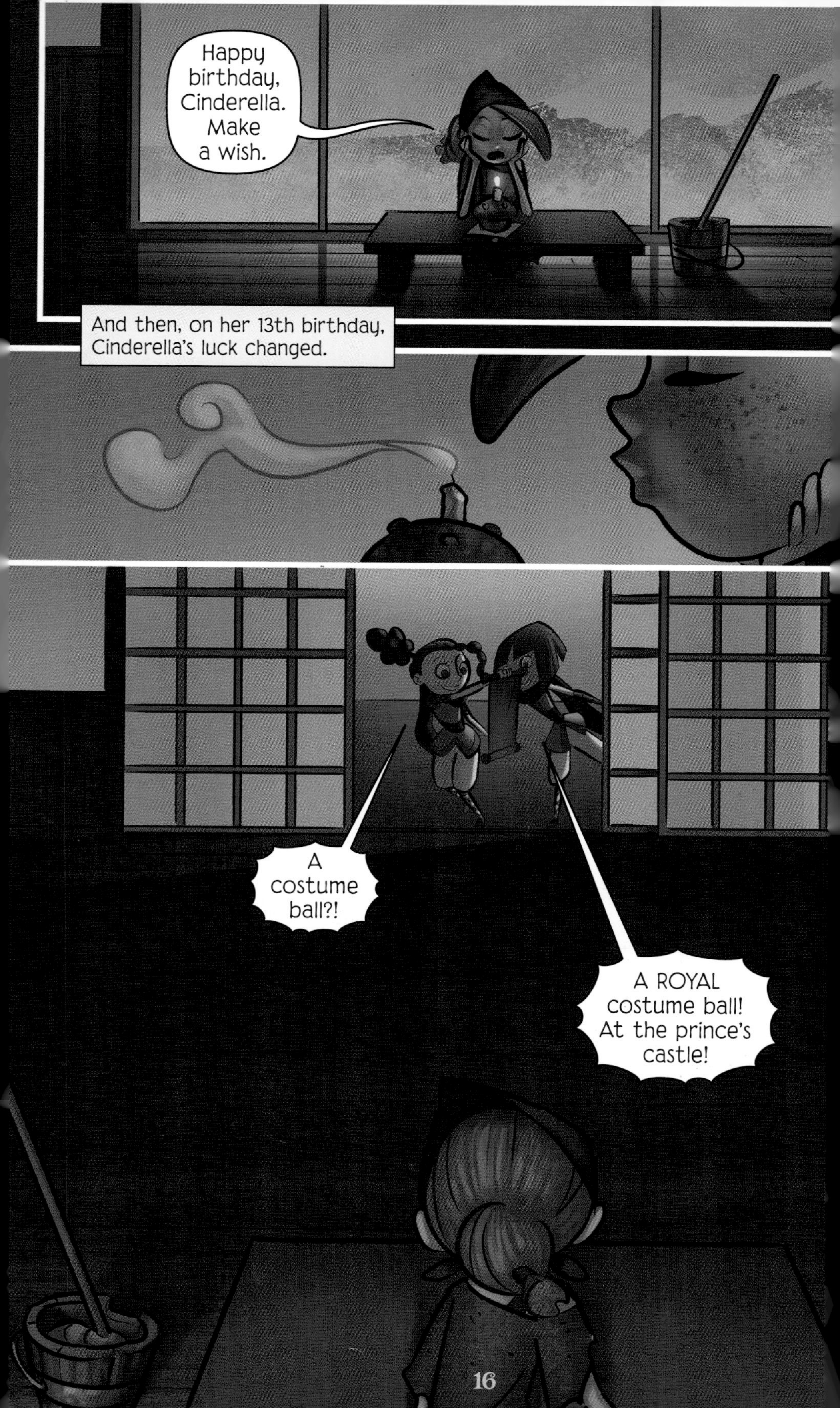

Happy birthday, Cinderella. Make a wish.
And then, on her 13th birthday, Cinderella's luck changed.
A costume ball?!
A ROYAL costume ball! At the prince's castle!

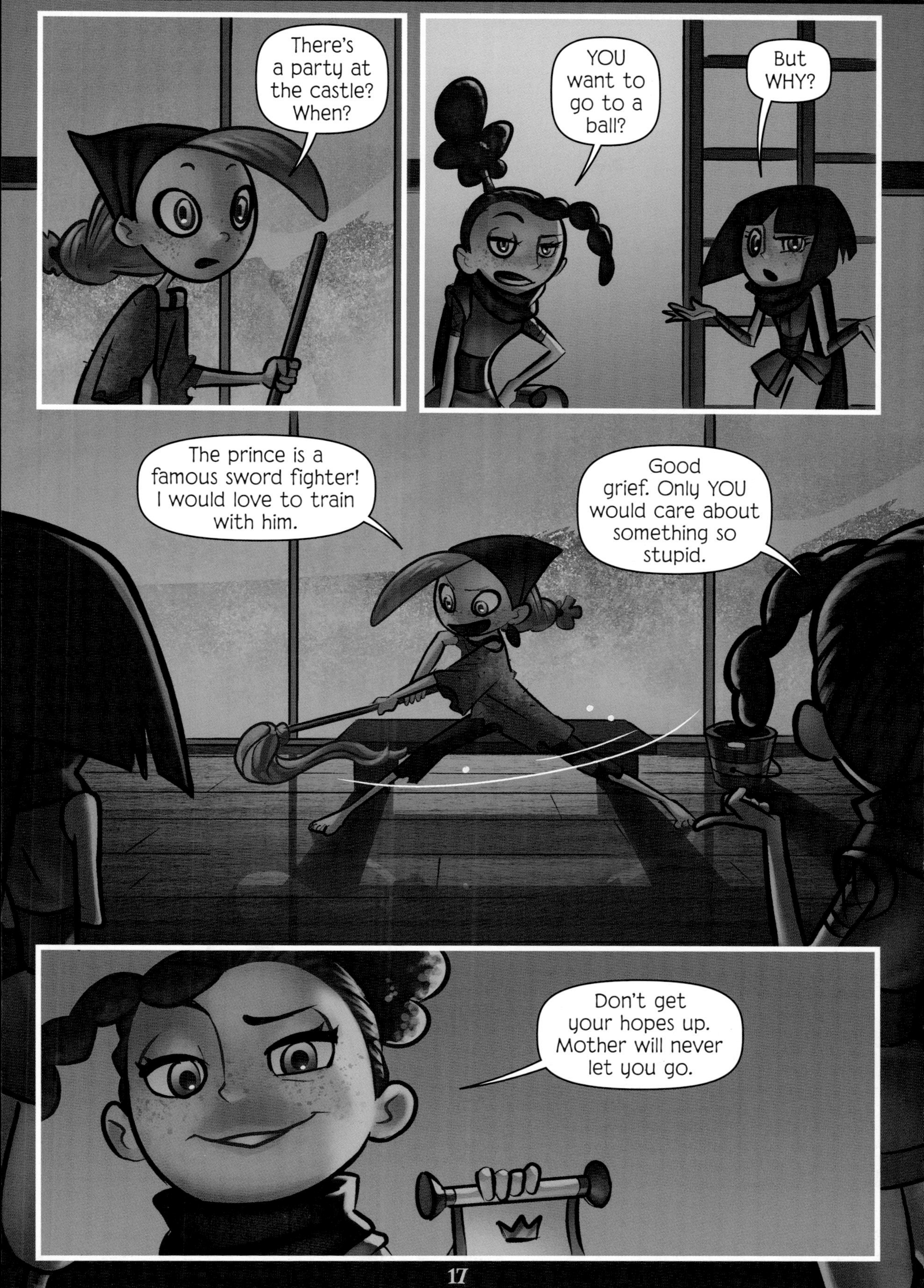
There's a party at the castle? When?
YOU want to go to a ball?
But WHY?
The prince is a famous sword fighter! I would love to train with him.
Good grief. Only YOU would care about something so stupid.
Don't get your hopes up. Mother will never let you go.

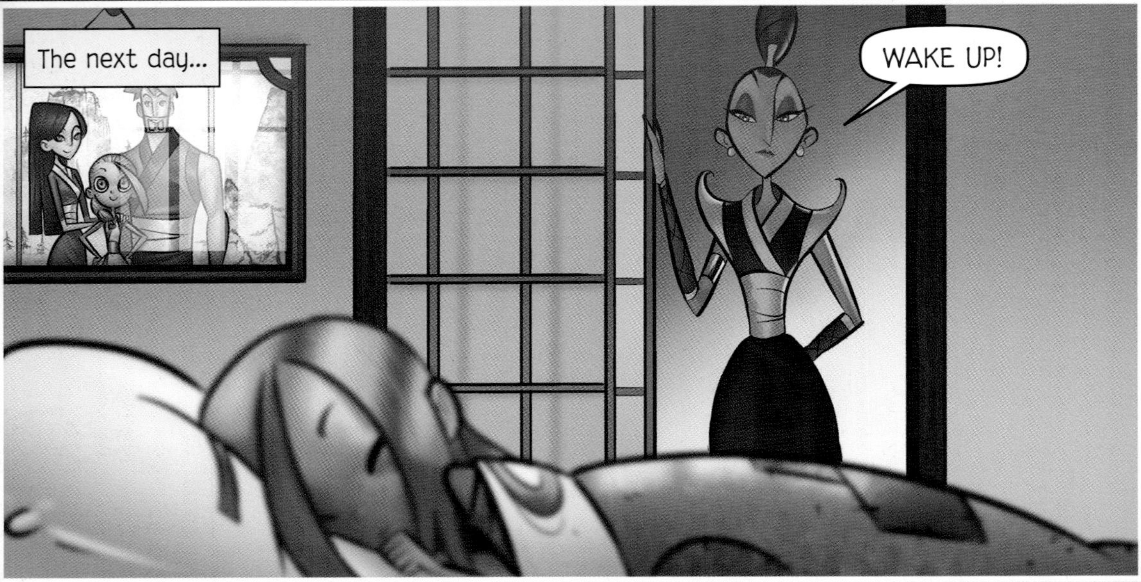

The next day...
WAKE UP!

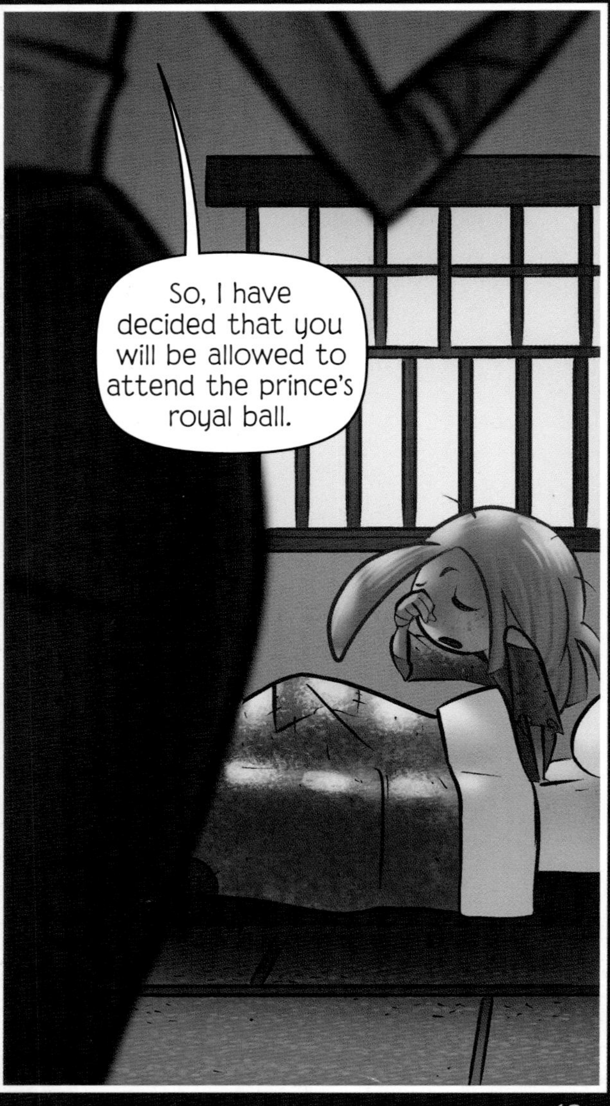

So, I have decided that you will be allowed to attend the prince's royal ball.

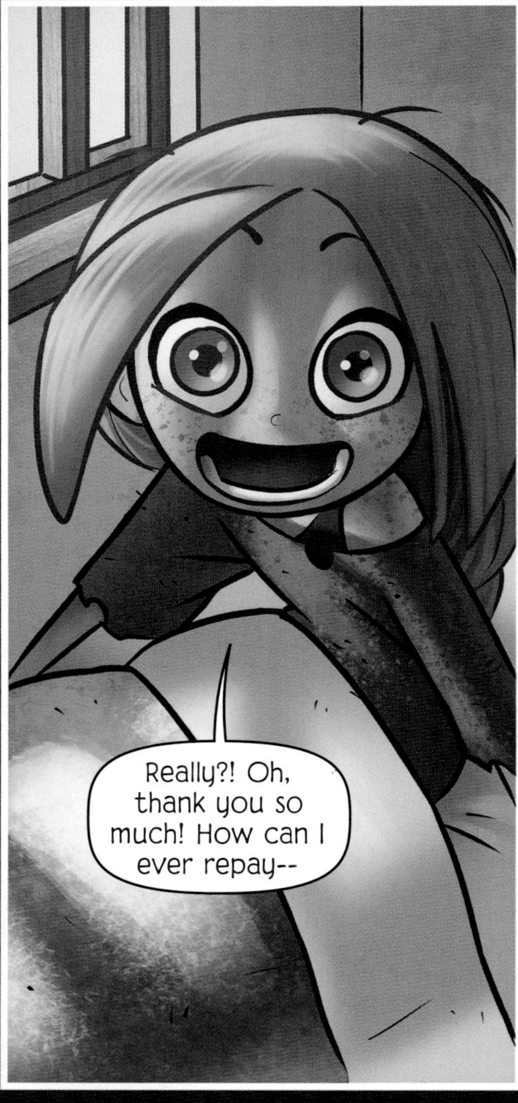

Really?! Oh, thank you so much! How can I ever repay--

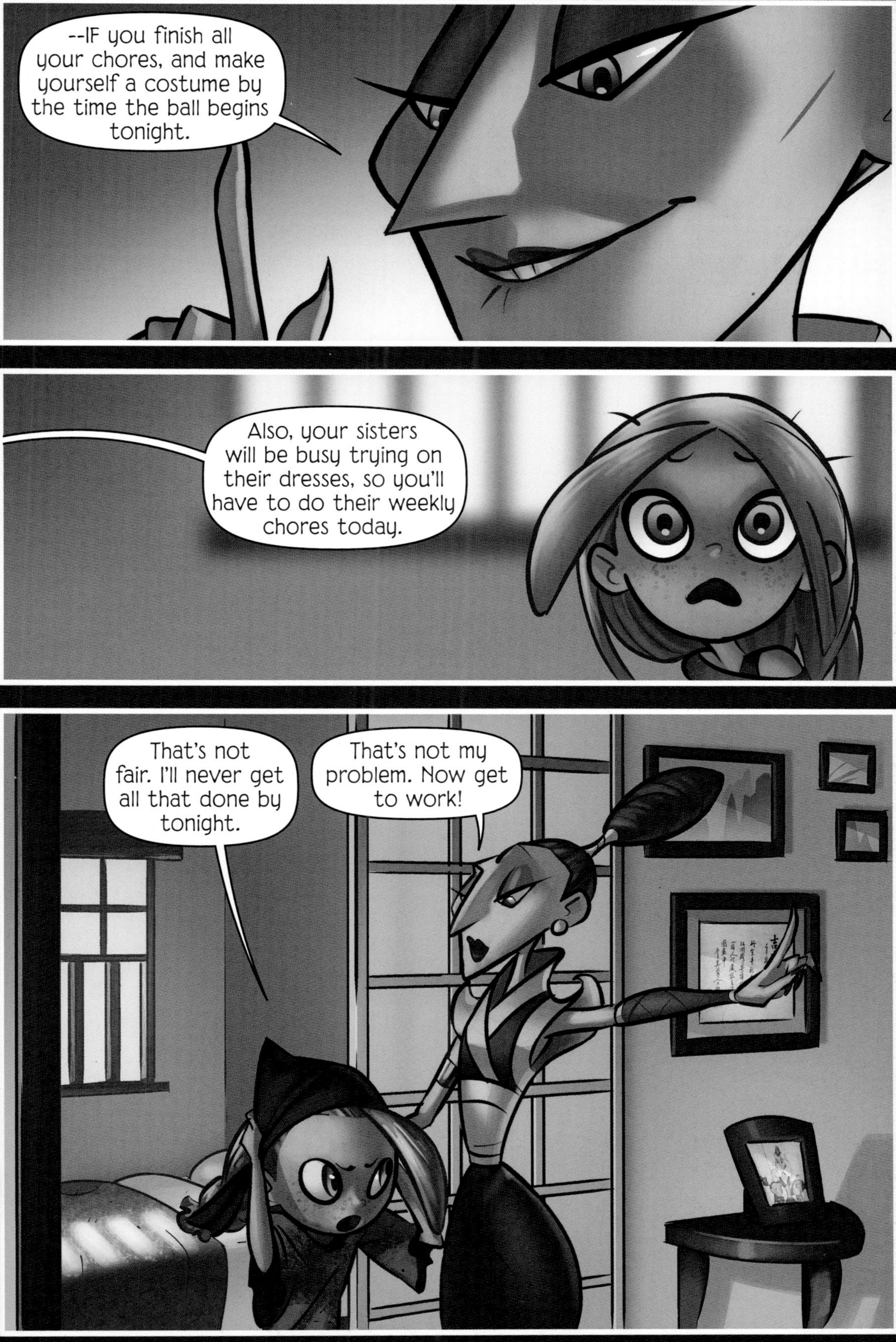
--IF you finish all your chores, and make yourself a costume by the time the ball begins tonight.
Also, your sisters will be busy trying on their dresses, so you'll have to do their weekly chores today.
That's not fair. I'll never get all that done by tonight.
That's not my problem. Now get to work!

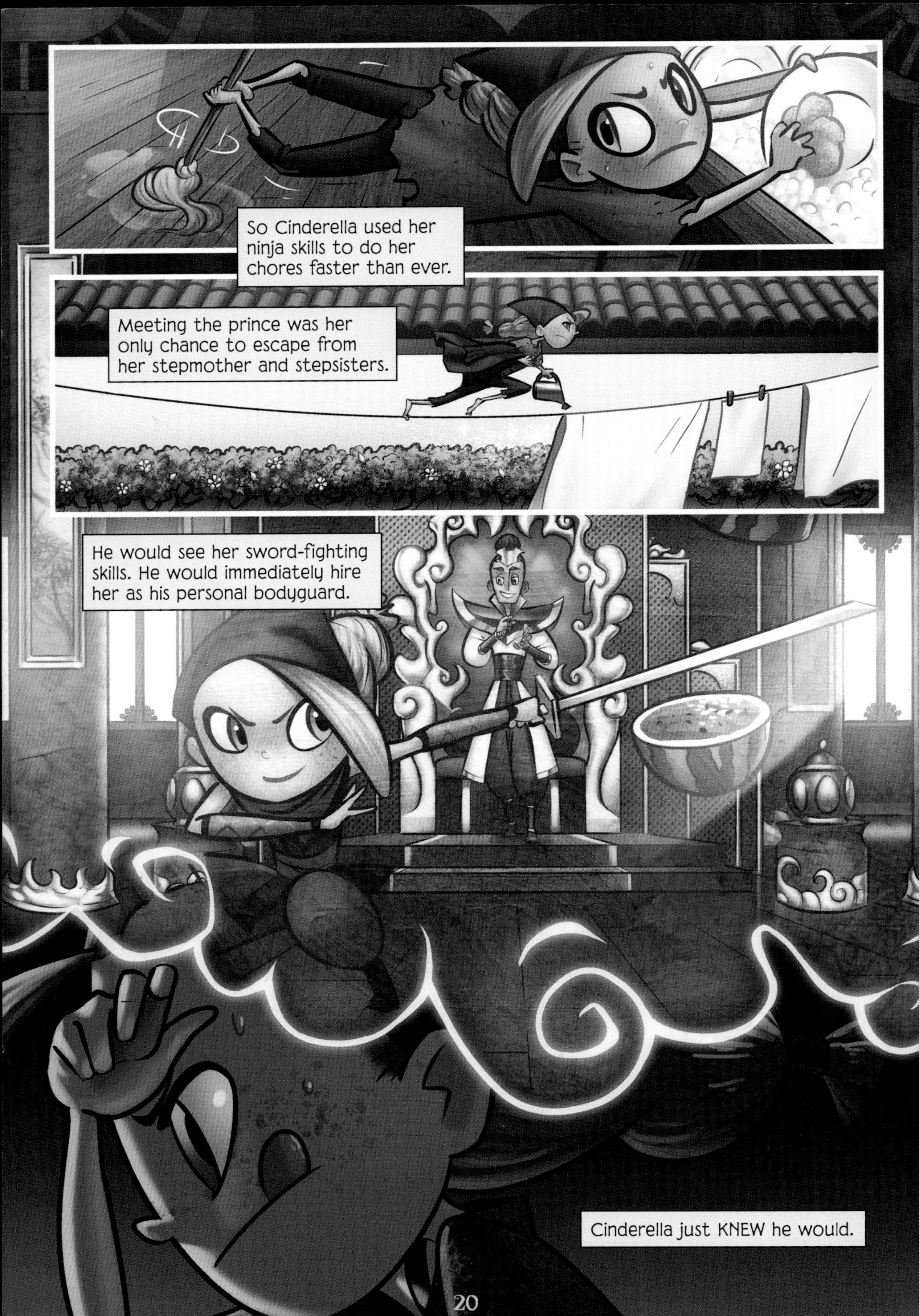
So Cinderella used her ninja skills to do her chores faster than ever.
Meeting the prince was her only chance to escape from her stepmother and stepsisters.
He would see her sword-fighting skills. He would immediately hire her as his personal bodyguard.
Cinderella just KNEW he would.

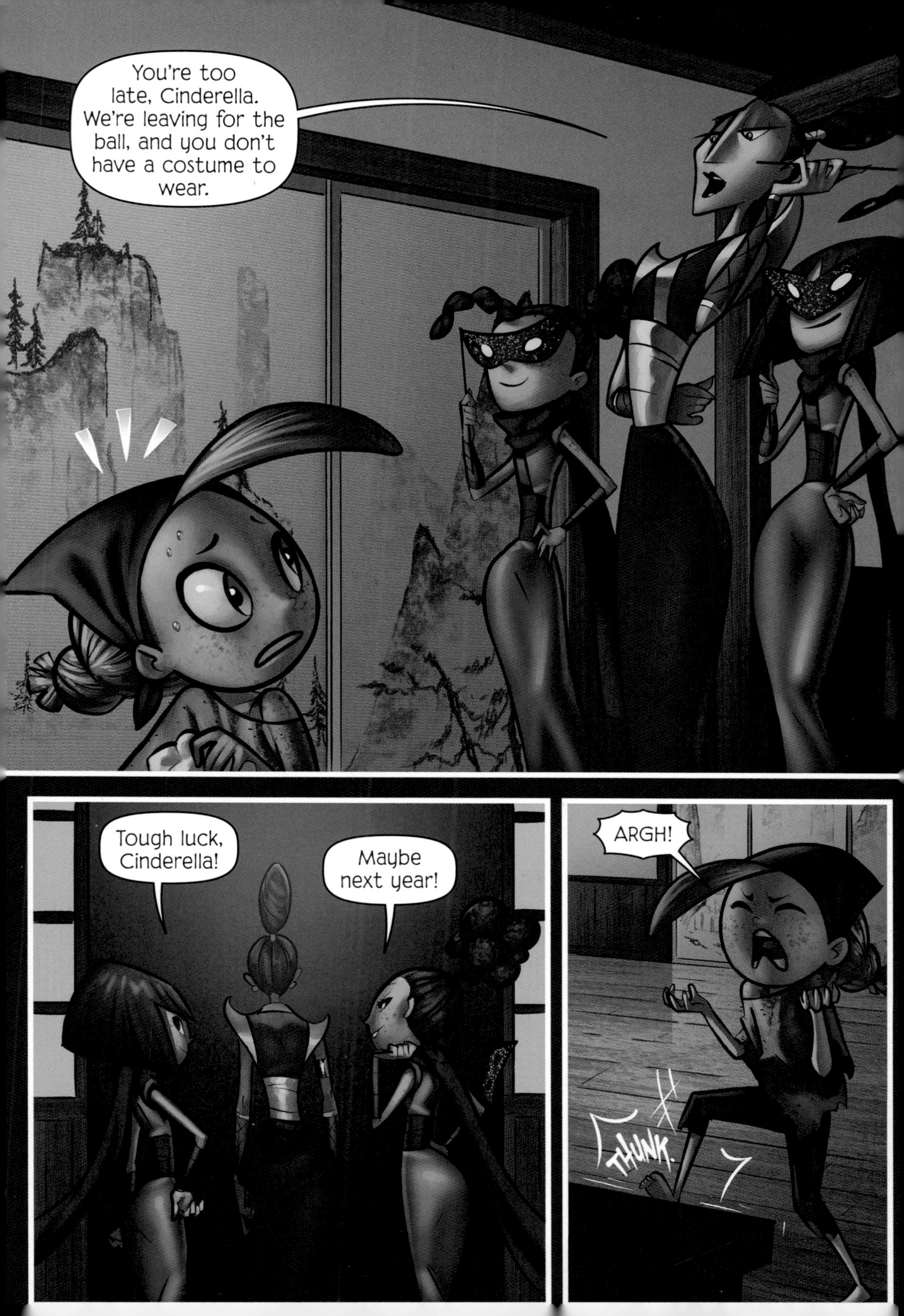
You're too late, Cinderella. We're leaving for the ball, and you don't have a costume to wear.
Tough luck, Cinderella!
Maybe next year!
ARGH!
THUNK.

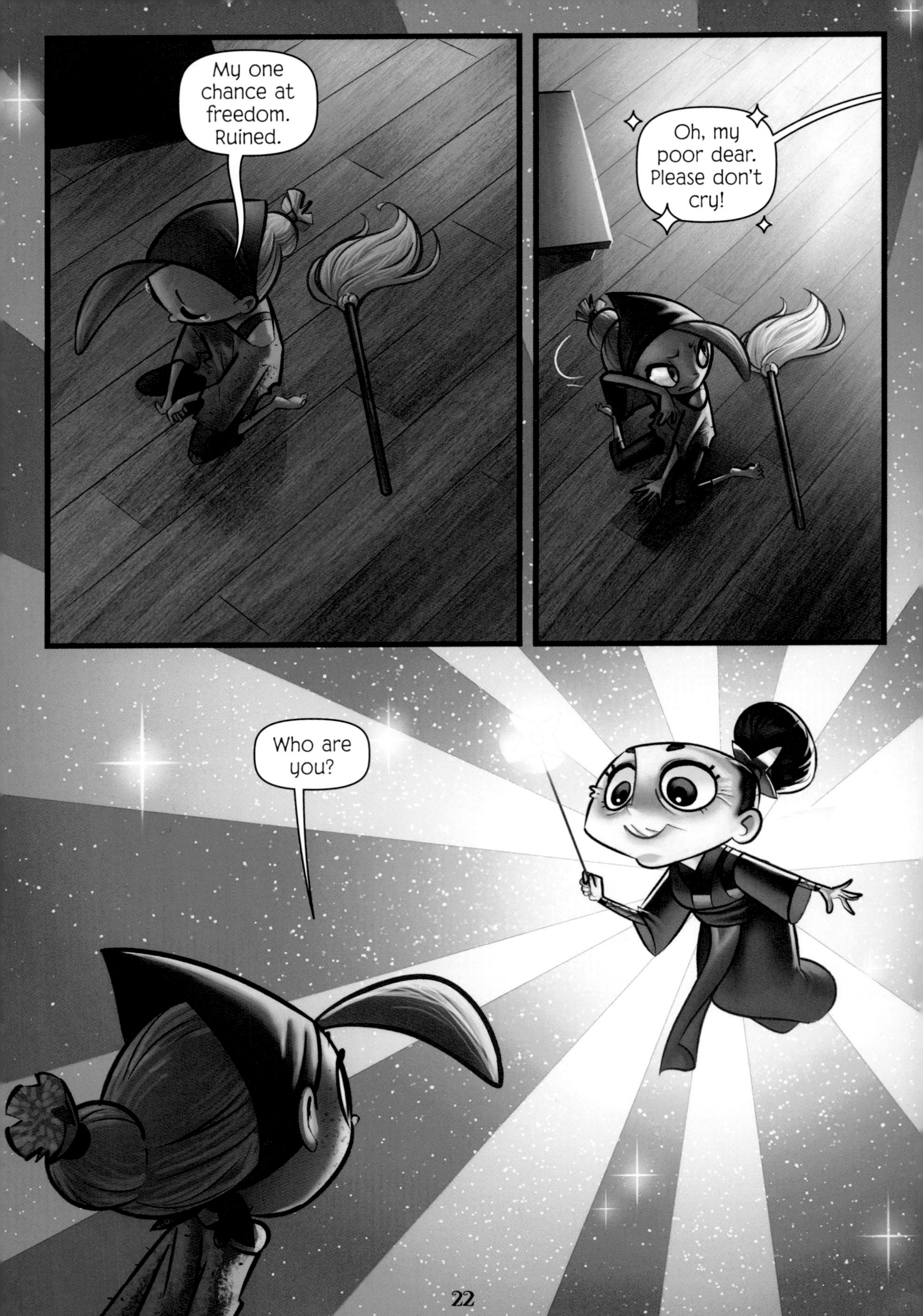
My one chance at freedom. Ruined.
Oh, my poor dear. Please don't cry!
Who are you?

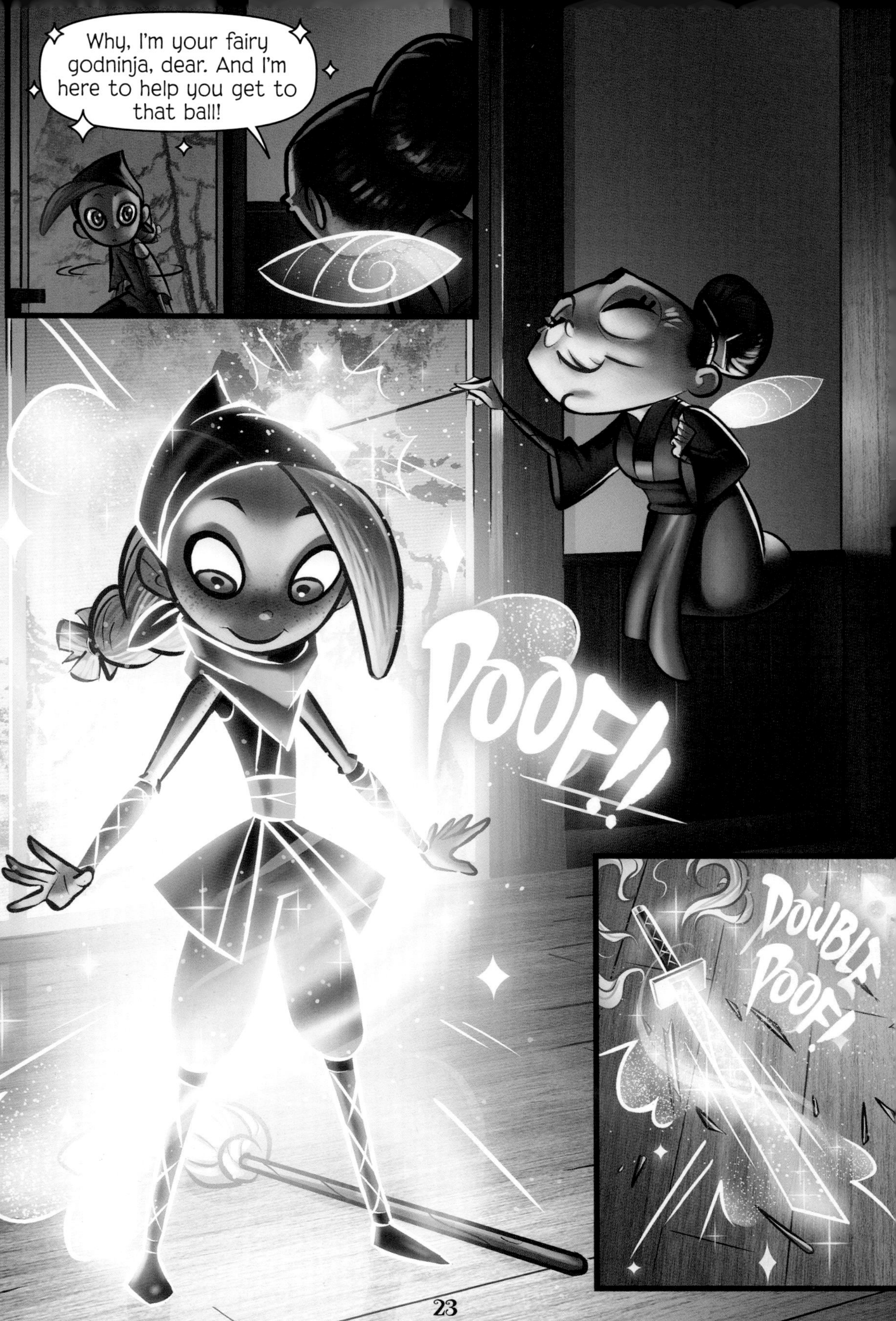

Why, I'm your fairy godninja, dear. And I'm here to help you get to that ball!
POOF!!
DOUBLE POOF!

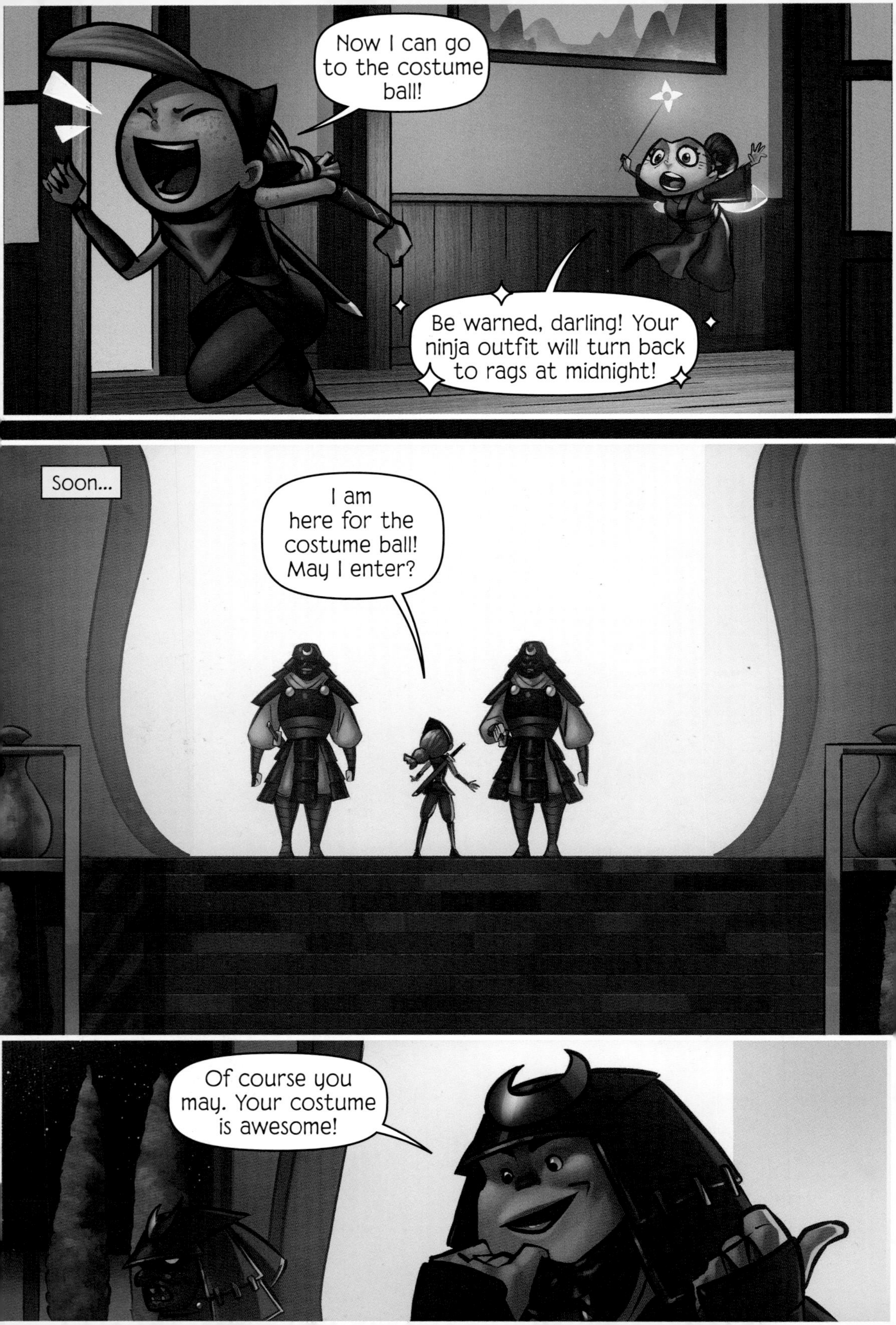
Now I can go to the costume ball!
Be warned, darling! Your ninja outfit will turn back to rags at midnight!
Soon...
I am here for the costume ball! May I enter?
Of course you may. Your costume is awesome!

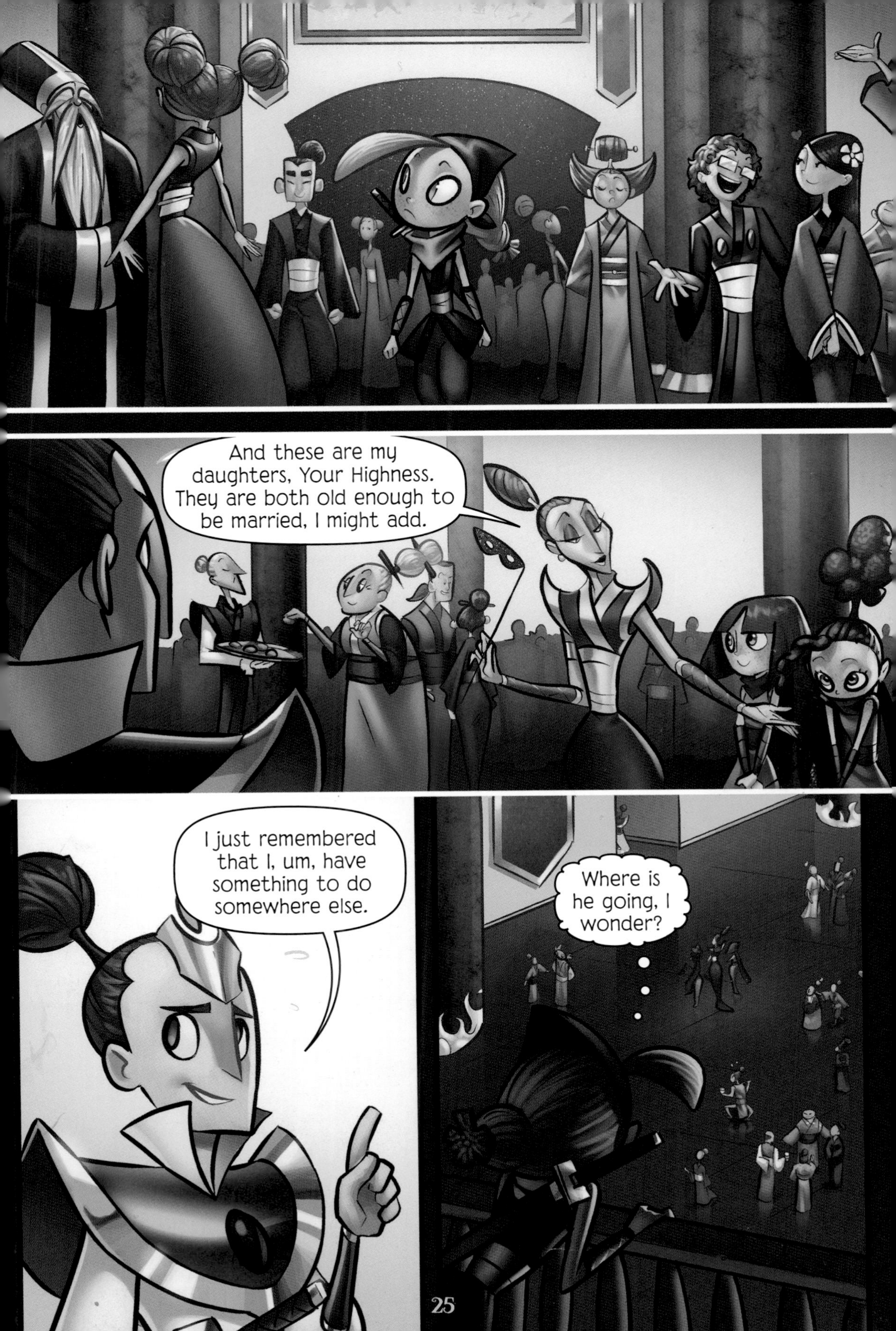

And these are my daughters, Your Highness. They are both old enough to be married, I might add.
I just remembered that I, um, have something to do somewhere else.
Where is he going, I wonder?

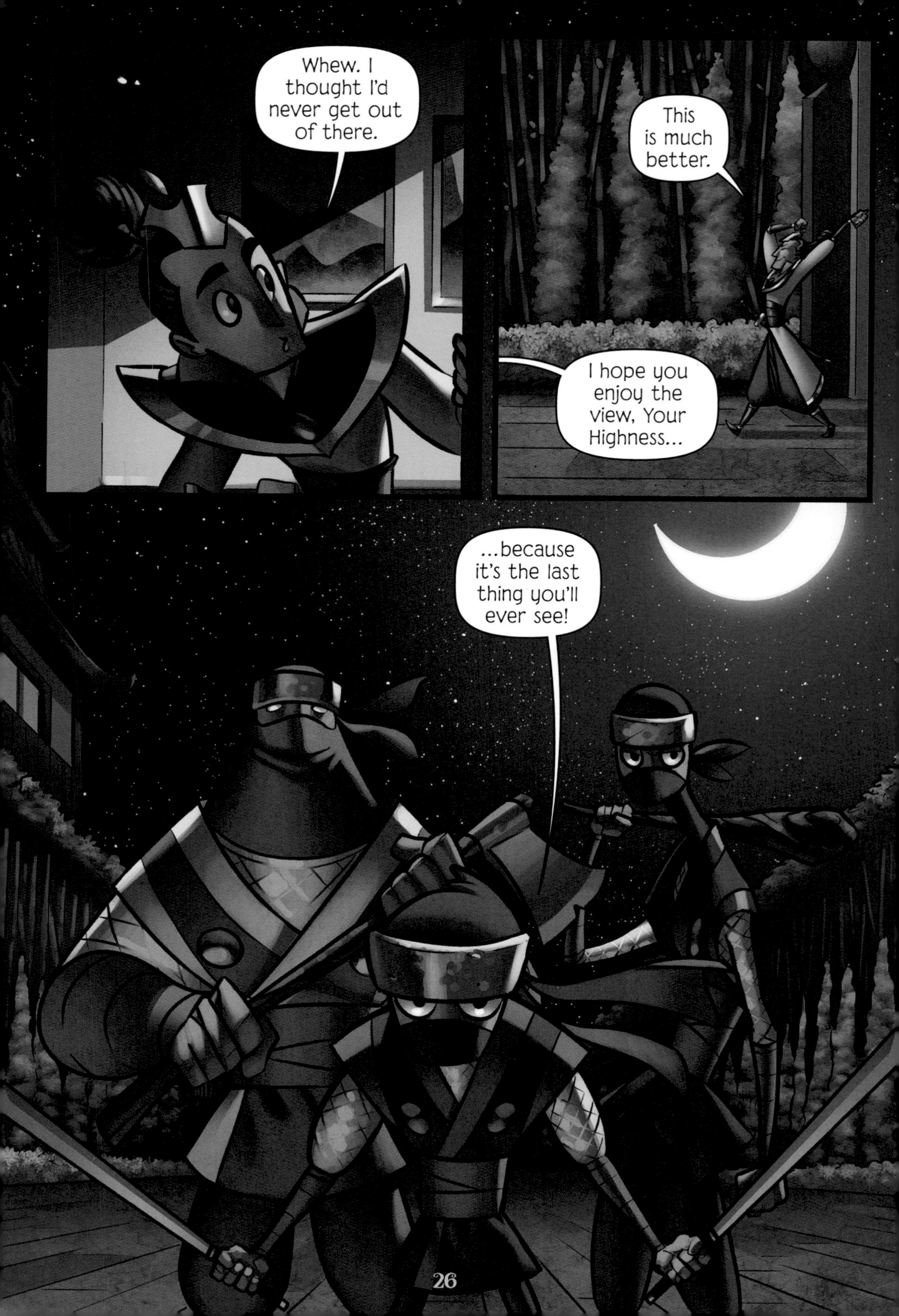
Whew. I thought I'd never get out of there.
This is much better.
I hope you enjoy the view, Your Highness...
...because it's the last thing you'll ever see!

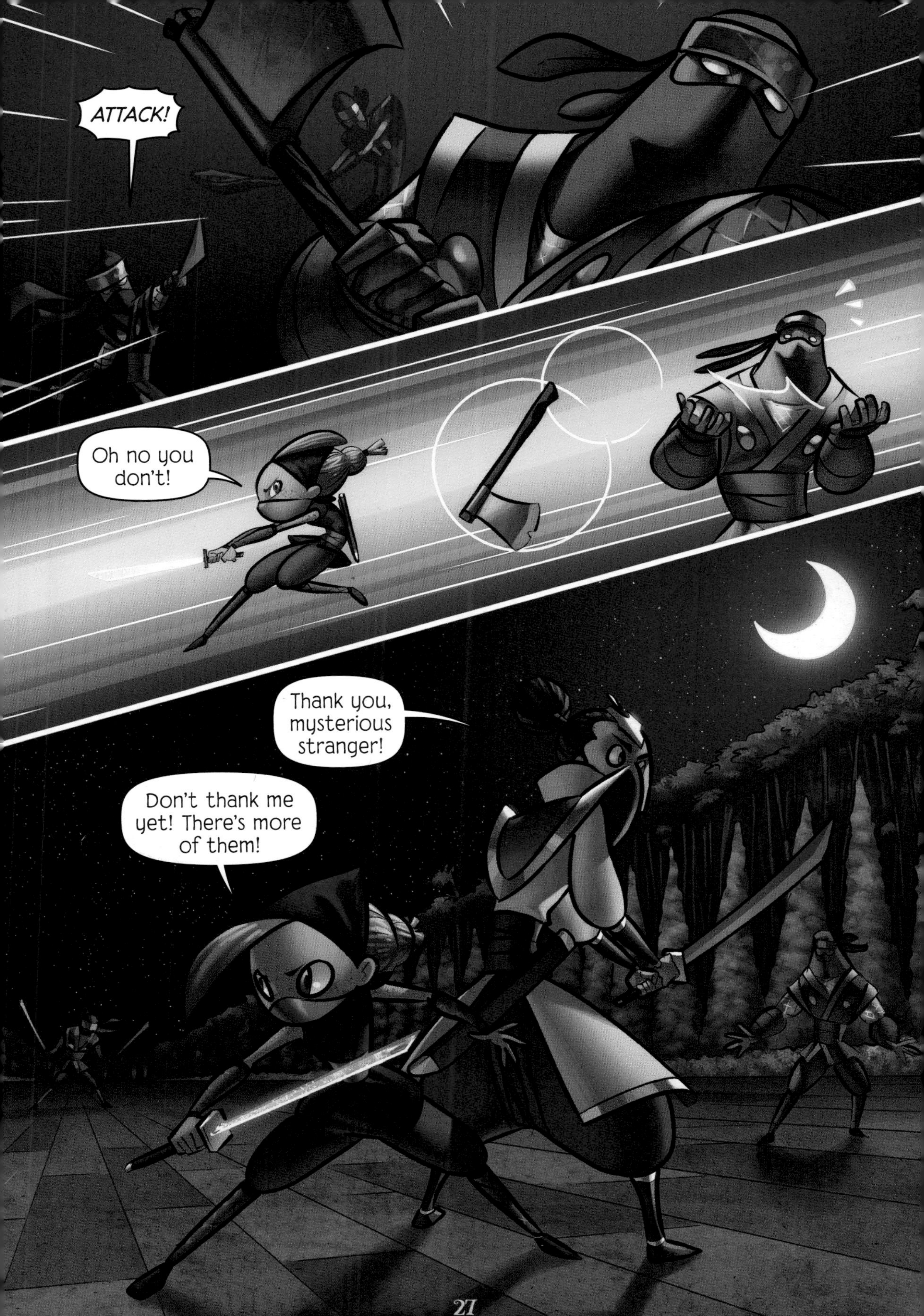
ATTACK!
Oh no you don't!
Thank you, mysterious stranger!
Don't thank me yet! There's more of them!

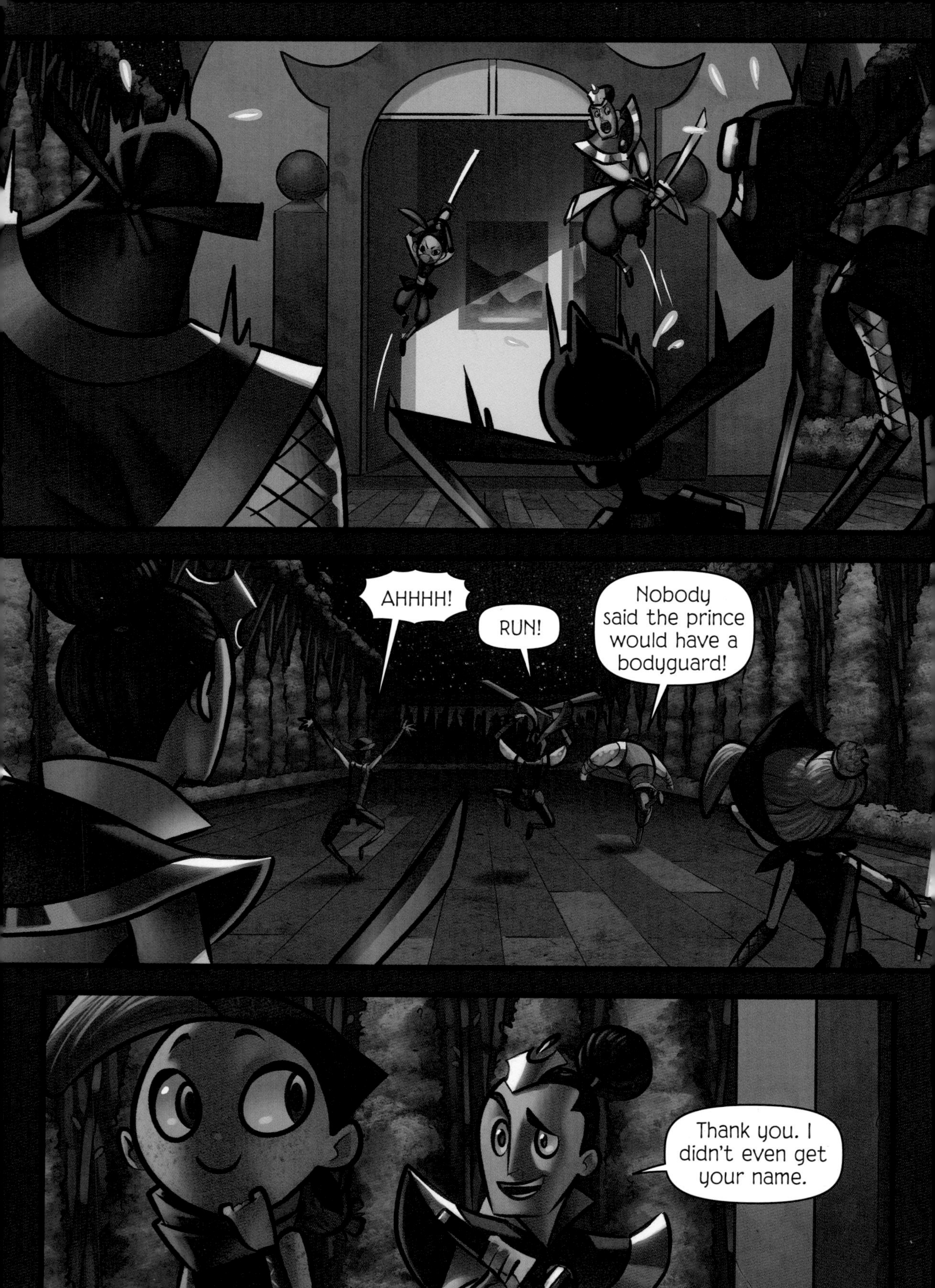
AHHHH!
RUN!
Nobody said the prince would have a bodyguard!
Thank you. I didn't even get your name.

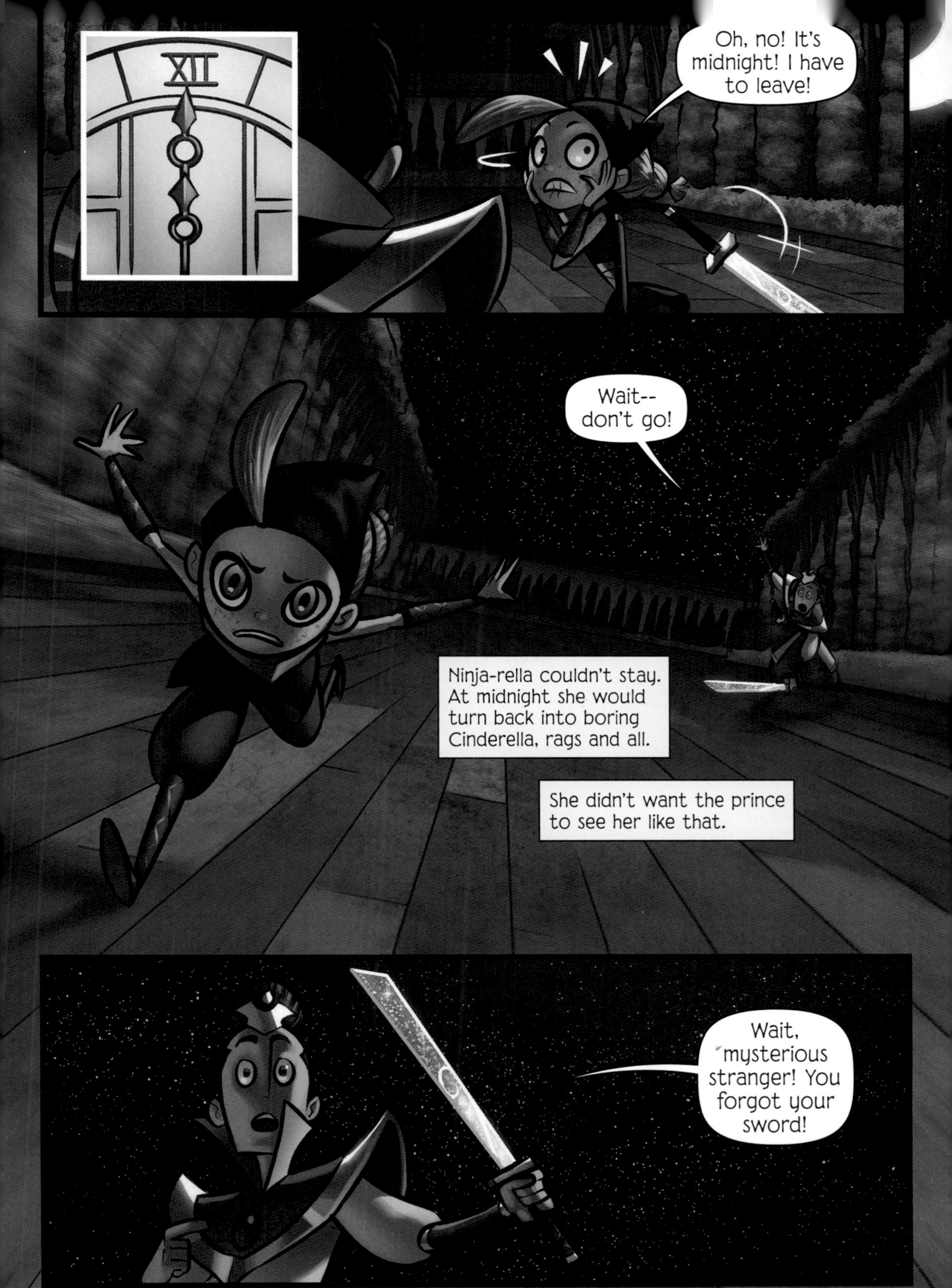

XII
Oh, no! It's midnight! I have to leave!
Wait-- don't go!
Ninja-rella couldn't stay. At midnight she would turn back into boring Cinderella, rags and all.
She didn't want the prince to see her like that.
Wait, mysterious stranger! You forgot your sword!

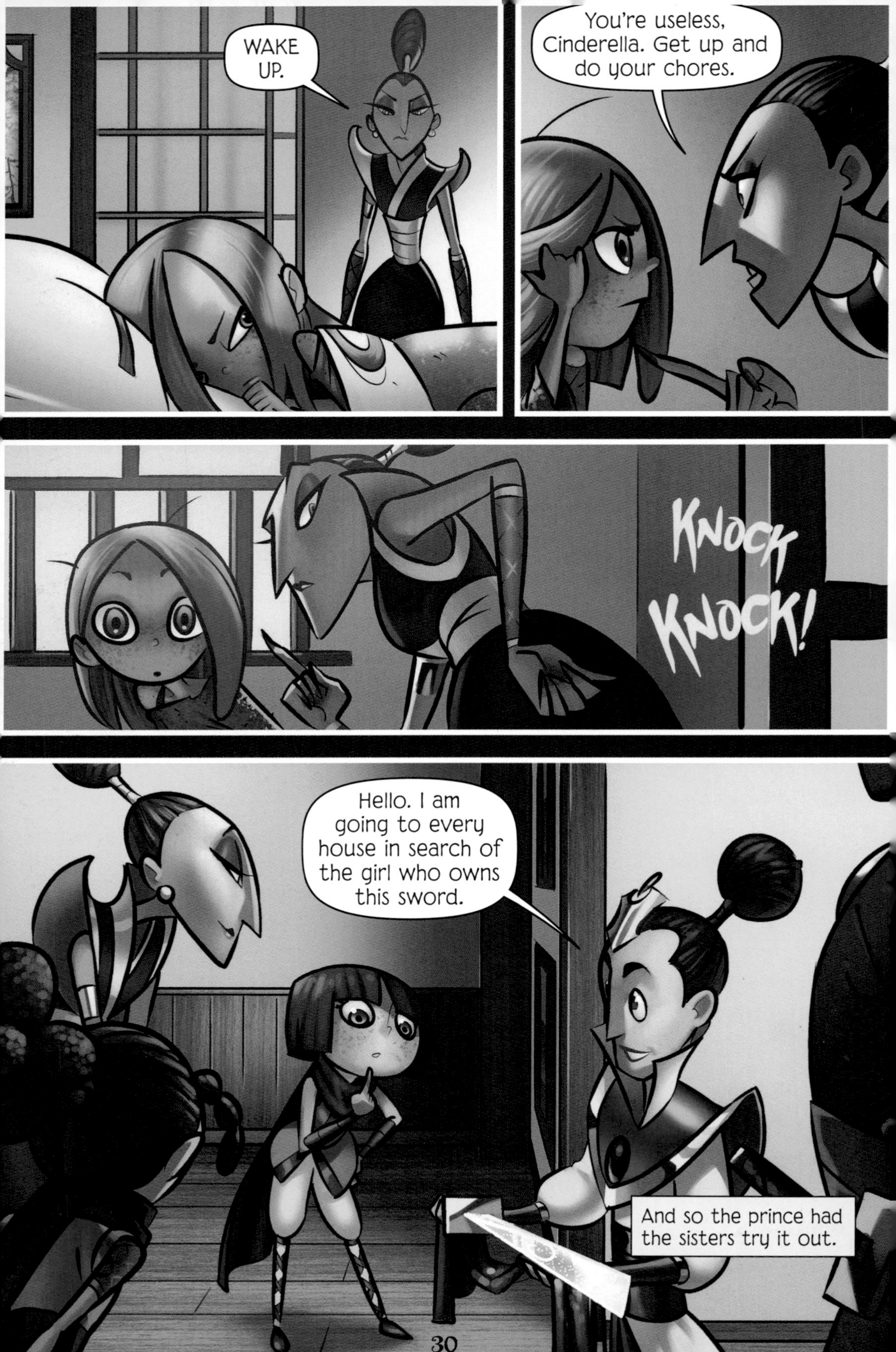

WAKE UP.
You're useless, Cinderella. Get up and do your chores.
KNOCK KNOCK!
Hello. I am going to every house in search of the girl who owns this sword.
And so the prince had the sisters try it out.

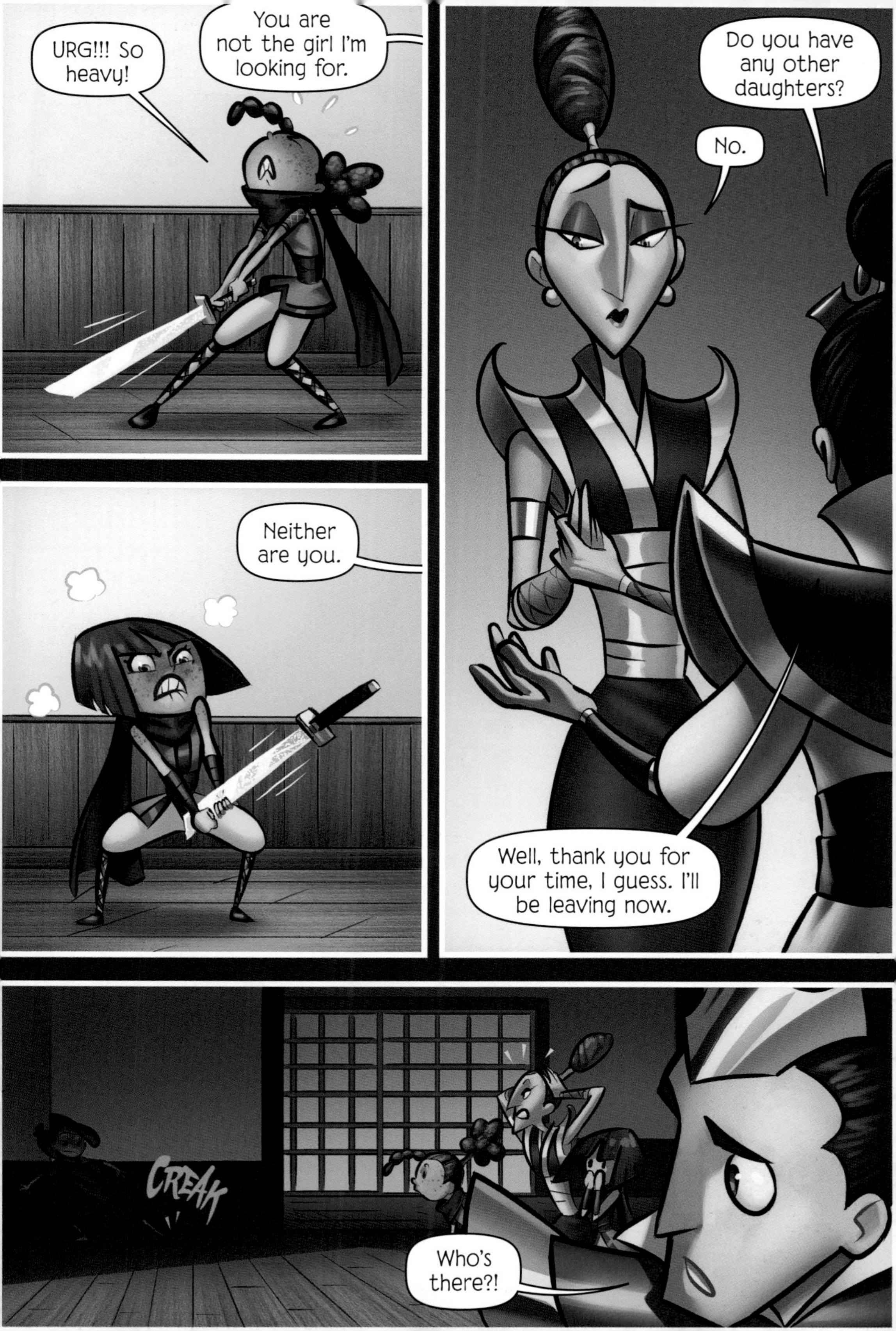
URG!!! So heavy!
You are not the girl I'm looking for.
Neither are you.
Do you have any other daughters?
No.
Well, thank you for your time, I guess. I'll be leaving now.
CREAK
Who's there?!

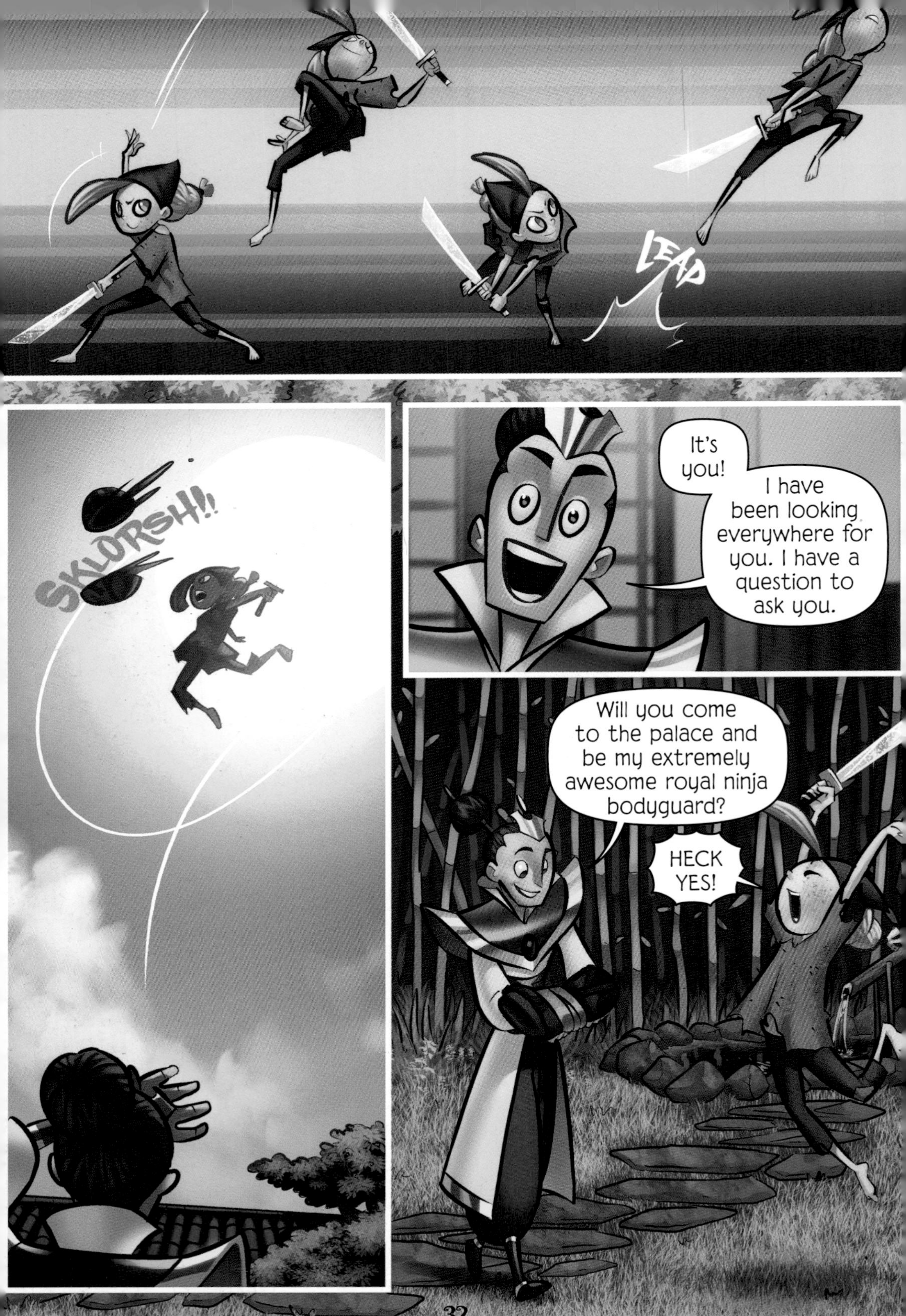
LEAP
SKLORSH!!
It's you!
I have been looking everywhere for you. I have a question to ask you.
Will you come to the palace and be my extremely awesome royal ninja bodyguard?
HECK YES!

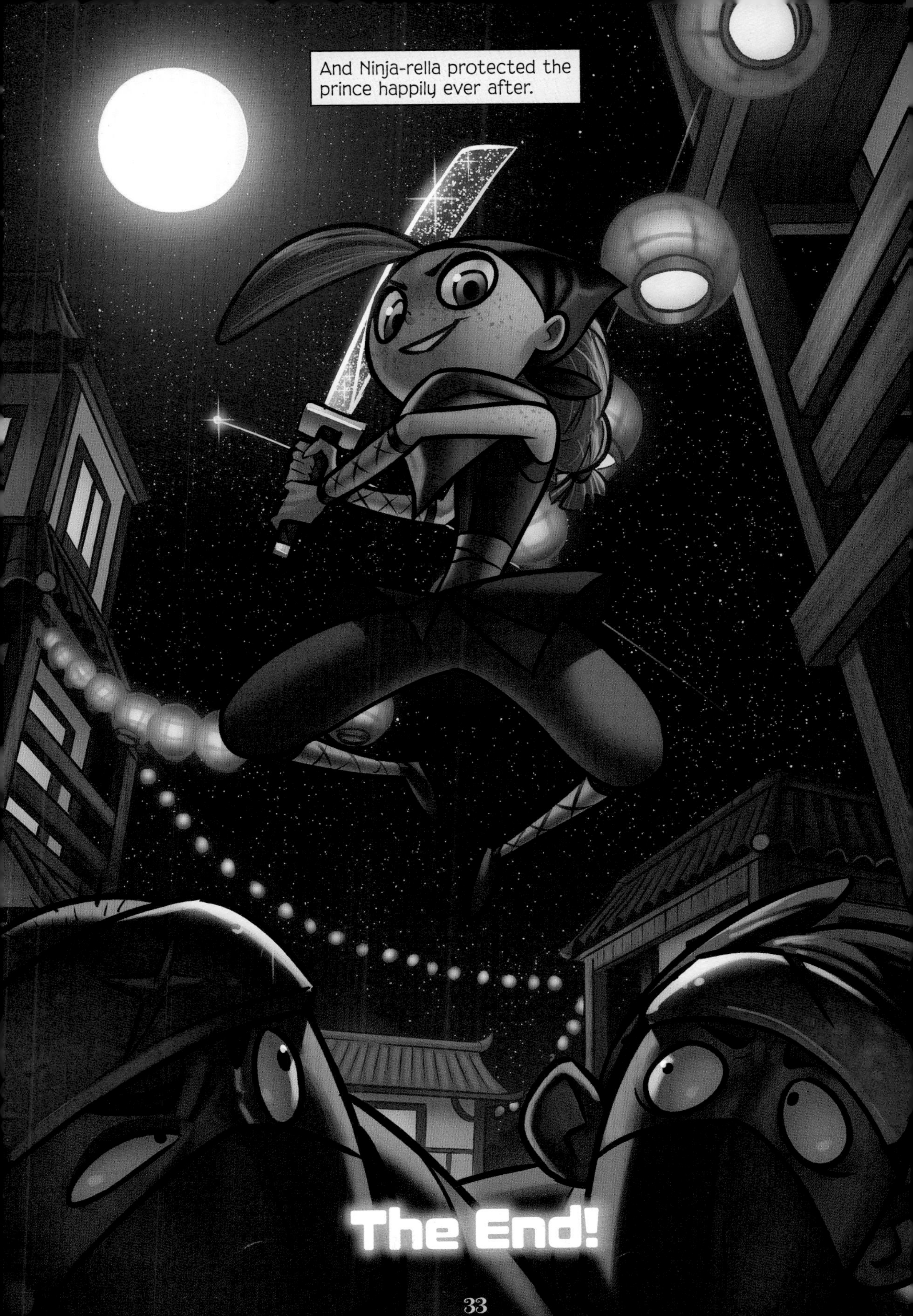
And Ninja-rella protected the prince happily ever after.
The End!

ALL ABOUT THE ORIGINAL TALE!

The story of Cinderella
has been around for ages.
The first popular version of
the tale was *Cenerentola* by
Giambattista Basile, published in 1634.
This Italian tale tells the story of a widowed
prince who has a daughter named Zezolla (Cinderella) who
convinces her father to marry her nanny. After the wedding, the
nanny moves in with all six of her own daughters. The stepsisters
treat Zezolla like their own personal slave, making the girl
miserable.

While traveling, Zezolla's father meets a magical fairy who gives
presents to him for Zezolla. He gives her a golden spade and bucket,
a silk napkin, and a small tree. Zezolla plants the tree and cares for it.
One day, a magical fairy emerges from its branches. To thank Zezolla
for taking care of her home, the fairy dresses Zezolla in beautiful
clothes and slippers so she can attend the king's royal ball.

At the ball, the king falls in love with Zezolla at first sight, but she
runs away before the king can find out who she is. Eventually, the
king's servant discovers one of Zezolla's slippers that she left behind.
So the king invites all of the ladies in the land to try on the special
shoe. When Zezolla draws near, the shoe jumps from the king's hand
onto her foot. They marry and live happily ever after.

Charles Perrault's version of the tale, *Cendrillon*, was written in 1697.
It includes the following additions: a magical fairy godmother, a
pumpkin-turned-carriage, and special slippers made of glass instead
of fabric!

Perrault's additions to the tale likely
made it more popular. To this
day, most adaptations use
his version of the tale,
including this one.

A **FAR OUT** GUIDE TO NINJA-RELLA'S TALE TWISTS!

Instead of wanting to marry the prince, Ninja-rella wants to be his bodyguard.

The fairy godmother of old is replaced by a fairy godninja, of course.

Instead of glass slippers, Ninja-rella gets a special glass katana sword!

And in place of a beautiful gown, Ninja-rella is given a sweet ninja outfit!

VISUAL QUESTIONS

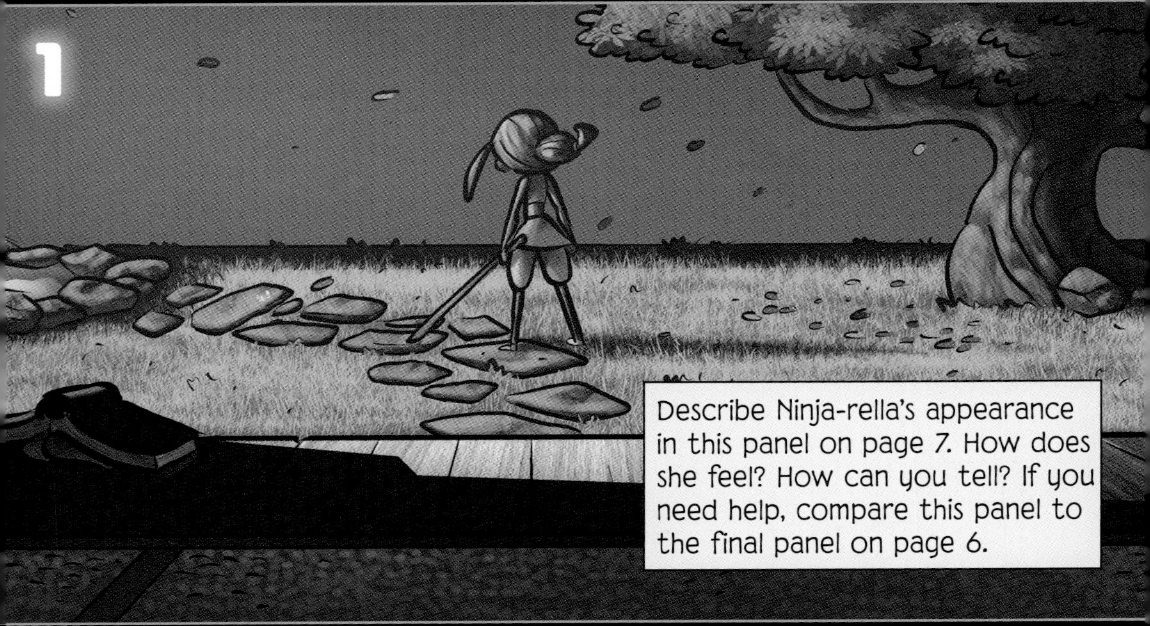
1
Describe Ninja-rella's appearance in this panel on page 7. How does she feel? How can you tell? If you need help, compare this panel to the final panel on page 6.

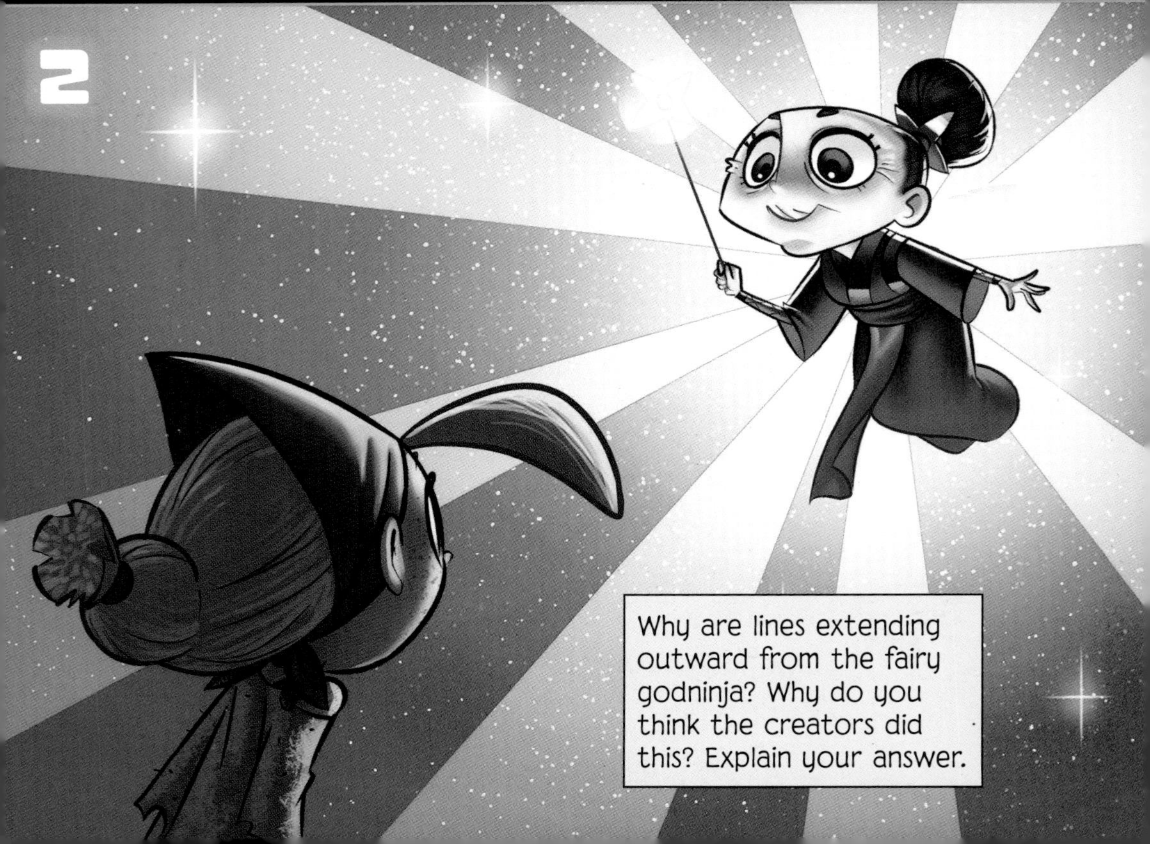
2
Why are lines extending outward from the fairy godninja? Why do you think the creators did this? Explain your answer.

3

In your own words, describe the path that Ninja-rella travels in this panel.

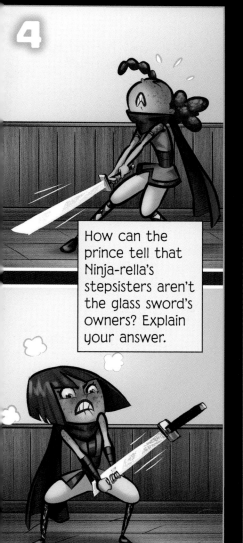

4

How can the prince tell that Ninja-rella's stepsisters aren't the glass sword's owners? Explain your answer.

5

The panels on this page are diagonal, or angled to the side. Why did the artist choose to draw the panels like this? How does it make you feel when you read it?

AUTHOR

Joey Comeau is a writer! He lives in Toronto, which is where he wrote the all-ages space-adventure comic *Bravest Warriors*. He also wrote the young adult zombie novel *One Bloody Thing After Another.* It's pretty spooky.

ILLUSTRATOR

Omar Lozano lives in Monterrey, Mexico. He has always been crazy for illustration and is constantly on the lookout for awesome things to draw. In his free time, he watches lots of movies, reads fantasy and sci-fi books, and draws! Omar has worked for Marvel, DC, IDW, Capstone, and several other publishing companies.

GLOSSARY

ball (BAHL)--a large and fancy formal party. Some balls, like costume balls, require all guests to dress as someone else or wear masks.

bodyguard (BAH-dee-gard)--a person whose job is to protect someone who is important, like a queen or a prince

chess (CHESS)--a strategic game played by two persons, each with sixteen pieces, on a chessboard. The goal of the game is to capture the other player's king.

godmother (GAHD-muhth-er)--a woman who serves as a female sponsor or guardian of a child

mere (MEER)--nothing more than what is stated

ninja (NIN-juh)--a practitioner of the Japanese martial art called ninjutsu. These warriors trained to be sneaky and strike quickly, usually at night.

ruined (ROO-ind)--destroyed, decayed, or spoiled

stepmother (STEHP-muh-thur)--a woman whom your father marries after his marriage to or relationship with your mother has ended. In fairy tales, stepmothers are often unfairly represented as evil and untrustworthy.

stepsister (STEHP-siss-ter)--the daughter of your stepmother or stepfather

useless (YOOSS-liss)--not useful at all, or of no worth or value